Thirty and single? Getcha ass to the Gathering!

Ugh. Gabriella Wickham thought turning thirty was bad enough, but now she's been invited (ordered) to attend this year's Gathering (werewolf speed dating). Having a Mark on her arm means that she's one of the few human women destined to mate with not one, but two Alpha werewolves. Thank goodness werewolves don't come in "ugly." After her sister Scarlet mates the Ruling Alphas, things really start to get interesting. Gabby runs into not one, but two hotter than hot werewolves who make her tingle in all the right places. Yum. Of course, "yum" comes with baggage of both the mental and female kind. Lovely. Luckily it's nothing a few punches and a good talking to can't cure. Maybe...-ish.

Berke Davis and Jack Wright know that lush, curvaceous Gabriella is their mate. Who cares that they're currently not part of an Alpha pair? Details, details. Burke has been half bound to his best friend Jack since they were four, but the past keeps them from solidifying their pairing and taking up the mantle of Alpha. Berke understands his friend's feelings, but Jack is about to get a lesson on living and loving. Berke just hopes the lessons are learned before they both lose Gabriella. Especially when she is Challenged by a rival to first blood...a Challenge that could end in very permanent, and deadly, consequences...for Gabriella.

CHAPTER ONE

Talk about an awesome souvenir. The organizer for the annual werewolf Gathering had purchased the best pens *ever*. Gabriella found them sitting in a pile on the registration desk, and she'd snared one before the morning's round of speed sniffing began.

Click.

Clickity click.

It had the perfect balance for her to spin it around her fingers.

Flip. Flip. Click. Click.

There was a brief pause and then she reversed the pen's path.

Clickity click. Flip. Click.

Okay, officially? She was engaging in various Tests of Proximity, not speed sniffing. Her sister Scarlet had called it werewolf speed dating.

So now she had to sit at a table opposite two chairs while Alpha Pairs made their way around the room. Then they'd sit, sniff, and go.

See? It boiled down to werewolf speed dating.

Well, they weren't only sniffing. There was this whole Mark thing going on, too.

Gabby sighed, hand automatically going to her left bicep. Stupid Mark. She'd been born with the thing. In a swirling triangular shape, the Mark was slightly darker than her overall hue and rose from her skin as if it were a scar. Present since birth, it signified her eventual mating to two— count 'em *two*—werewolves.

Which left her lounging around enduring the Test of Proximity with pair after pair while the one wolf who'd caught her eye lurked outside the ballroom. A glance toward the doors revealed that the man still skulked, moving like the predatory animal that prowled just beneath his skin.

Too bad she couldn't mate a single wolf. Nope, individual wolves, those that weren't Alphas and part of an Alpha Pair, mated other wolves and never humans. Only pairs ended up with a human Marked as their mate.

Except…except her Mark had reacted to the Captain's presence. It'd heated and throbbed and screamed at her to rush into the wolf's arms. Supposedly that only happened when a Marked was around the ones meant for her.

Funny how the guy she reacted to wasn't part of a pair. He seemed dominant enough. But he was the Captain of her newly mated sister's guards, which meant he was definitely not paired up and ruling a Pack.

Geez, her sister now had *guards*. Gah. Scarlet had not only mated the previous night—their first night at the Gathering—but she'd snared the North American Ruling Alphas: Keller Aaron and Madden Harris. Which left Scarlet out of the morning's activities and Gabriella all alone.

Lucky (maybe) bitch.

Low chimes filled the air and then the shift of bodies relocating replaced the gentle sounds. Oh, look, time for the Alpha Pairs to move on to the next "lucky" (she almost snorted) lady.

Gabby sighed as she saw her next two potential mates approach.

They weren't bad looking, like, at all. It seemed shifters didn't come in ugly. Nope, they were all tall, muscular and gorgeous. While she, Gabriella Wickham, was short, plump and rather ordinary. Good thing a big part of mating was based on her Mark's reaction and not the men's attraction to her.

She sighed and was thankful her sisters couldn't read her thoughts. They'd spent her entire life bitching at her about her Debbie Downer attitude when it came to men. They kept trying to convince her that men could love her just the way she was, big butt and all.

The two newcomers slid into the seats across from her, all predatory smiles and leers. God, were wolves this hard up that they were looking at her with sex on the brain?

Whatevs.

Pasting on a purely fake smile, she held out her hand. "Hi, I'm Gabriella Wickham. My friends call me Gabby."

Knowing what was coming, she kept her expression frozen in place. The first guy didn't even bother to introduce himself. Nope, he gently gripped her hand and brought it to his lips. Actually, his nose. The first time it'd happened she'd nearly swooned at the seductive gesture. She'd thought the wolf was going to brush a kiss across her knuckles like some gallant man of old. As if. The guys were really taking a good whiff to see if she belonged to them.

He turned her hand over and slid his nose along her inner-wrist, sending chilly air rushing over her skin. The seductive light in his eyes instantly dimmed.

Yeah, she could have told him she didn't belong to them. The Mark on her bicep wasn't doing jack shit. No pulse-y ache, no heat, no throbbing of her pussy that said "Ooh, take me now!" None of it.

But the guy didn't seem eager to brush her aside. Still silent, he handed her off to his other half, and that man cradled her hand within his, bringing it to his nose to give her the same treatment. The hint of desire in this other man's gaze immediately lowered to casual appreciation.

He released her slowly, and she pulled her arm back to her side.

Wow. Silent.

"So, you are…" She let her question go unsaid, but still the Alpha Pair remained quiet, their lips pressed together until they formed thin, white lines. Now their bodies vibrated with barely suppressed agitation. So, they wanted to get on their way now that they knew she wasn't their mate. "Okay then."

Gabby slumped back into her chair and resumed her pen spinning.

Flip. Flip. Click. Click. Clickety. Click.

The stupid *ding* hadn't sounded yet. Damn it. Movement to her right showed a smiling trio rising from their seats, hands clasped and moving away from their table. The two men enfolded the woman in a hug, hands roaming as they embraced her. A glance around the room revealed that all eyes were on the trio, looks of fierce longing on every male's features.

Gabby huffed out a breath, suddenly reminded of the wolves' nature. The Alpha Pairs could lead happily without their Marked, but couldn't rule indefinitely unless they had a woman to offset their violent tendencies. She would calm and soothe their beasts so that life in a Pack became a lot less bloody.

That was part of the reason for the rules that every Marked had to abide by. They all had to agree to entertain requests for Tests of Proximity to see if they were meant for an Alpha Pair. Another rule was that, if a Marked hadn't found her mates by her thirtieth birthday, she was forced to attend the Gathering. Hey, guess who'd turned thirty, like, a week ago? Ding! The Wickham triplets!

The law regarding the Gathering was one thing they'd all forgotten about along the way. Well, it was actually just she and Scarlet since they were the only two that'd been born with a Mark. But somehow Whitney had gotten an un-declinable invitation. Which was something Gabby and Scarlet still needed to investigate somewhere in between rounds of Gabby's sniff-me-baby-one-more-time at the Tests of Proximity and Scarlet's sessions of gimme-gimme-more with her Ruling Alpha mates.

More action drew her gaze to another table: another trio rising and moving from the room, a woman grinning between two wolves.

5

Dude. When was she gonna get that? Sure, she put up a kick ass front about not wanting a ménage mating. But the more she saw Scarlet's happiness and the shining smiles in the grand ballroom, the more she craved finding her own two guys.

They'd want her, and her alone, unable to cheat because wolves mated for life, and would (hopefully) be patient when it came to sex since she (apparently) sucked at it. How many men had called her frigid by now? Gabby rolled through the list in her mind. *The last was Allen. Charlie before him. Zeke? Or was it Xavier? Gah, they sounded alike.*

The low *ding* came again, sending the Alpha Pairs into action. As one, the remaining sets rose and moved on to the next table. Her empty chairs suddenly filled with another couple of strangers.

Without a word or hesitation, she stuck out her arm, wrist bared, and waited for them to take a sniff.

It was going to be a very long, agonizing day.

*

It was going to be a very long, blood-coated day.

Berke Davis paced outside the hotel's grand ballroom, taking a moment to peer inside with each pass. She was there, right *there*, every time he looked inside. And surrounded by Alpha Pairs.

God damn it.

Berke had to take comfort in the fact that she was destined to belong to him—him and Jack—whether the other wolf liked it or not.

He ached to go to her, to march into the room and yank her away from those wolves. Somewhere deep inside, he knew that the luscious Gabriella Wickham belonged to him and him alone. Well, not alone. There was Jack…

Berke shook his head. One thing at a time. First he needed to get Gabriella away from those unmated wolves. Another Alpha gripped Gabriella's wrist and brought it to his nose.

That was it. That wolf would die. Slowly. Painfully. No one touched what belonged to him and—

"Captain?" A female voice interrupted his thoughts, the single word oozing sex and a promise.

He squeezed his eyes shut and sighed. Sometimes he hated his duty. Hated the fact that, because he was the Ruling Alpha's Captain of the Guard, he had to play nice with the attending staff and their families. Sliding his features into an expressionless mask, he turned toward the owner of the sexualized purring voice. "Hannah."

The female wolf closed the distance between them, seduction in each sway of her hips. Once upon a time, he'd have found her blatant invitation intriguing. Hell, he would have taken her up on it and enjoyed their time together. But now he'd found Gabriella and was determined to claim her. There were still hurdles to overcome, but there was no doubt in his mind that the curvaceous Marked was his.

A delicate hand stroked his chest, the red-painted nails scraping against the numerous medals that adorned his uniform. "I haven't seen you lately." She paused and eased closer. "Berke." His name rolled off her tongue in an unjustified familiarity.

He gritted his teeth and bit back his snarl. His wolf growled within his mind, warning him to cease the female's touch before the beast pushed its way out and did it for him. Grasping her wrist, he removed her hand from his chest and took a step back before releasing her.

"I've been engaged with the Ruling Alphas. You are aware of this." He did his best to soothe his wolf. They wouldn't tangle with this one. She wasn't their Gabriella. "What do you need?"

Hannah simpered, a tiny flash of hurt filling her eyes as she poked out her lower lip. "I thought you and I could..."

The rustle of moving bodies drew his attention away from the woman and back to the ballroom. Alpha Pairs and the Marked were all rising from their tables, the din of their voices growing with each passing second. The morning Tests of Proximity were done, and they were breaking for a brief lunch. Based on the Alpha Mate's schedule... No, she'd told him to call her Scarlet. Right. Well, based on *Scarlet's* schedule, his Gabriella would be dining with her sisters at one of the hotel's restaurants.

Berke cut Hannah off. "Unfortunately, I'm on duty." He turned his back on her, gaze scanning the growing crowd in search of his quarry.

"Maybe we can get together later. You, me, Jack..."

He rolled his eyes and glanced over his shoulder. As if his best friend and Lieutenant would be up for her once he met

8

Gabriella. Right now Berke just needed to get away from this woman and on his Marked's tail. "Yeah, maybe."

It'd taken some fast talking to get permission to guard Gabriella since he was the Captain and not some normal soldier. At breakfast that morning, he'd first laid eyes on the delicious woman. He'd let his gaze trail over her curves, taking in every inch of her seductive body, and he'd burned. His cock had gone instantly hard while a heat seared his left bicep. He'd rubbed the spot, watching avidly as she did the same.

Before he could take a step toward the woman, the Ruling Alphas had appeared and taken him away. His wolf roared and snarled its objections but submitted to the much stronger pair. From there it became a battle of wills, the Ruling Alphas adamant in their protection of their mate's sister while he was just as determined to claim her. Unfortunately, they wanted to keep him from her while he wanted to keep everyone else away.

Eventually, he'd won. Or rather, the Ruling Alphas had tired of arguing with him and could no longer be from Scarlet's side. They'd rushed off to be with their mate and he'd rushed...here.

Spotting his destined within the crowd, Berke went on the move, weaving through Alpha Pairs and Marked alike as he fought to keep her within sight. He knew her destination; he just needed to ensure she arrived safely. Nothing was more important that Gabriella. Nothing.

The throng grew, thousands of bodies pouring into the massive hallways of the hotel. Their voices echoed off the marble flooring and against the high ceilings.

His Marked wove and strode amongst the gathering, dancing farther and farther from his position. Using his massive bulk, he pushed past Alpha Pair after Alpha Pair, ignoring the grumbles, snarls, and growls that trailed behind him. Some appeared to take exception, their glowing yellow eyes focusing on him, but a curve of his lip and flash of fang quickly subdued them. No one wanted to tangle with the Ruling Alphas' Captain of the Guard. He was respected and feared in nearly equal measure, and he readily admitted that he liked the fact that fear won out every once in a while.

Berke caught up to Gabriella just as she dashed into the upscale restaurant. Two of his guards were stationed at the entrance, and they both nodded at her appearance. They lived only because their gazes didn't linger on her body.

Keeping his distance, he slipped into the dim space behind her. If he got too close, she'd sense his presence, for without a doubt, her Mark would respond to him just as it had that morning. But he couldn't approach her or woo her, until he settled the issue of not being part of an Alpha Pair.

Details.

Splitting his attention between Gabriella and the room at large, he spotted his quarry: Lieutenant Jack Wright. The moment his Marked settled at the table with her sisters Scarlet and Whitney, he diverted his course. His Lieutenant was stationed along the wall, body tense and watchful as he surveyed the room.

Jack focused on Berke and straightened, coming to attention. "Captain."

Berke shook his head. "Jack, we need to talk."

10

The wolf's eyes narrowed, immediately suspicious. "Captain, I'm not sure what we need to discuss."

His beast growled, not caring for the man's aggression and tone. Jack was an Alpha through and through, but so was he. "We need to *discuss* the future."

"There's nothing to say, Captain." The last word was practically spat at him.

This argument was an old one. Berke would say they needed to talk about their status as single wolves instead of an Alpha Pair. Jack would get defensive because Berke wouldn't just "leave it alone." Eventually, it'd all end in a fight capped off with a few beers. They were men. It was what they did. Misunderstandings equaled anger equaled bloody fights and then beer.

Sometimes an Alpha just needed to get his fang on. But Jack wasn't an Alpha. Right.

"Fine." Until now he'd kept Jack on the periphery of assigned duties. Berke had been expected to remain at the Ruling Alphas' sides, which meant the next senior officer needed to corral the rest of the guards. "Go relieve Hawkins by the Sisters Wickham." He smirked then, imagining what was to come for his oldest friend. "After lunch, you'll be responsible for Gabriella. I'll meet you outside of the ballroom around two. She's got a few more hours of Proximity testing this afternoon."

Berke's wolf wasn't happy about leaving Gabriella, but Jack needed to face the truth for himself.

The two of them were Alphas.

11

Together they were an Alpha Pair.

Even better, Gabriella Wickham was their Marked mate.

*

Jack Wright glared at his retreating commander's back, unsure of the wolf's intentions. Through their partial bond, he could sense smugness in the man, a feeling of joy mixed with cockiness, and that worried him. Still buried beneath that was the too familiar pain of their stilted connection.

Like a coward, he pushed those emotions aside. Their life was fine just the way it was. There was no reason to upset the status quo with dreams of a different future. His wolf snarled inside him, pacing and clawing at him as it always did, telling him without words how wrong his thoughts were.

What did the beast know?

Brushing aside his irritation, he navigated to the Ruling Alpha Mate's table. Scarlet was an animated woman, full of energy and sass. Something the Ruling Alphas seemed to appreciate. He'd already heard rumblings about amending laws regarding the Marked women and how they were treated. Some of the Alpha Pairs he'd encountered were less than thrilled with Scarlet, but Jack admitted that he respected the woman. She'd walked into an unknown situation, hitched herself to the most dominant wolves in North America, and was already making changes.

She was definitely a worthy mate to the Ruling Alphas.

The distance between Jack and the sisters lessened with his every step. All three of them were talking at the same time, arms and hands waving, their happiness and joy evident on their faces.

He shook his head, grin teasing his lips. Yeah, the Ruling Alphas, and the future mates of the other two sisters, would undoubtedly have eventful lives with the Wickham women.

In reality, the jury was still out on whether or not Whitney would end up with an Alpha Pair. She was human and had been summoned to the Gathering like all other Marked, but she didn't actually *have* a Mark. He knew this from overhearing some of the sisters' ranting, and apparently the Wardens were on the women's menu. Those two wolves were responsible for summoning Marked to the Gathering, and Scarlet was ready to skin them alive for forcing her sister to attend. Yeah, he didn't envy those men. Good thing the pair had been delayed. Maybe the trio would calm a little before the Wardens arrived.

The guards surrounding the Alpha Mate's table all had smiles on their faces, vigilant yet enjoying their duty. Okay, maybe watching these three wouldn't be so bad.

Jack changed his path and headed toward Hawkins, the man standing to the left and in front of the shared table, just behind Gabriella Wickham. At least he'd be in a good position to protect her.

A wave of scent assaulted him, forcing his steps to stutter, and he wobbled to catch himself. Pure sin and sweetness filled his nose, the flavors so seductive they went straight to his cock. Heaven, pure and simple.

He tipped his head back, inhaling deep and hunting for more of that alluring aroma. It was…there! He caught it and ventured forward, attention split between his original destination and that—cinnamon?—goodness. Yes, cinnamon and sugar with a hint of apples. God, apple pie. Mixed in were the unmistakable hints of pure woman. Those scents twining together called to Jack's wolf like nothing ever before. The beast surged forward, determination in its every shift of muscle. The powerful animal raced beneath his skin, sending pinpricks of pain along his arms. His fur lurked near, shoving at his control.

But still he hunted. The source wouldn't evade him. No way. Not when he knew that she was his, his mate, his one.

With this realization, Jack relaxed and released some of the pain he'd been harboring. He'd found his mate independent of Berke. They *weren't* meant to be an Alpha Pair after all. Just as he'd believed for years, they had never been destined to form an Alpha bond and then find their Marked. No, because he'd discovered his other half, not other third. He wouldn't have to suffer like his father, wouldn't have to harm innocents or...

The familiar woodsy scent of a wolf wasn't present in the fragrance he chased, but it didn't mean anything. She could simply be a human-wolf mix. Single wolves could mate with a mixed, right? He wasn't sure. Damn it, where were the Wardens when he needed them? They harbored the werewolves' knowledge and magic and could answer his question without thought.

Jack stumbled and bumped into a chair, tripping over the occupant, yet he managed to catch himself on the table before he sent them both tumbling to the ground. Oh, it was much stronger now. It was his mate trapped beneath him, her body so near his.

14

The flavors of cinnamon, apples, and woman intensified, threatening to overwhelm him and tear down his last remnants of control. He was touching her, their skin only separated by their clothing, and he ached to strip them bare so he could claim her. The woman had to be a wolf—single wolves could only mate with other wolves—and she would understand and relish in his public claiming.

Yes, he'd tear off her clothes and—

"Lieutenant?"

He knew that voice. He should listen to it. He should... But his female was half beneath him, his body sheltering her as he loomed above her.

"Lieutenant, quit your growling and let my sister go. Bad wolf." There was power behind the woman's words, but his wolf tossed them aside.

"Mine." He pushed the word past his lips, forcing a human syllable from his mouth. The wolf still fought him.

"No. Bad puppy." The voice was sharp.

"What are you gonna say next? 'Sit?' Really?" Those sarcastic, lyrical words were followed by a snort, and then the woman under him shifted and pushed at his chest, nudging him away.

Unacceptable.

Jack growled and stiffened, not allowing his mate to brush him aside. He had to make a stand now before she gathered the mistaken impression that he was a pushover. He let his small displeasure roll through his chest, travelling from his limbs and into the woman. Damn, his mate was small, much smaller than him, and his body easily covered hers.

"Lieutenant." The word was snapped, power flowing over him with every syllable and he recognized the source, the flavors of the dominance. It tasted like the Ruling Alphas, softer yet no less powerful than the wolves themselves.

Fuck.

Jack's wolf demanded that he ignore the Alpha Mate, take what belonged to them and squire her back to their den. But his life would be forfeit if he denied Scarlet's command.

Taking a deep breath, he begged his beast to recede and give him some measure of control. Once they were done with the Alpha Mate, they could run with their female.

He pushed back from the table and straightened, forcing his gaze toward Scarlet. It took no time to find the woman as she was seated directly across from him, a small smile playing on her lips. None of the anger he'd sensed before showed in her features. No, she was decidedly amused.

A glance around him revealed why.

Six guards surrounded Jack, all of them his friends and subordinates. Not an uncommon occurrence. Except normally they weren't aiming their guns at him. He let his gaze slide over pistol after pistol, the muzzle of each one pointed at his head. Twelve in all were trained on him.

Raising his hands, he fought for calm, urging his wolf to retreat while he figured out how to keep them alive long enough to claim their mate. Slowly he returned his attention to Scarlet. "Alpha Mate?"

The woman smirked. Her attention drifted to the woman before him and then back to his face. "Lieutenant, I don't believe you've met my sister, Gabby."

Scarlet's sister.

Her sister Gabriella.

Gabriella who was Marked, and the woman he was to escort back to the grand ballroom for further Tests of Proximity.

"Fuck."

Running. Running would be good right about now.

Because he wasn't an Alpha.

He wasn't part of an Alpha Pair.

And Gabby was definitely not his mate.

Too bad his wolf disagreed.

*

Berke sensed Jack's approach, recognizing the emotions clouding his friend's mind. Rage roiled within the other man, the feeling overriding everything he'd experienced in the last ten minutes.

Apparently his friend wasn't going to follow orders and was hunting him down immediately.

He'd left the Lieutenant with his command, but had hung around long enough to see Jack find their mate's scent. He'd stumbled along and located their Gabriella, and that was when he'd made his retreat. The other wolf needed the opportunity to face what he'd been denying since they were young.

Jack was an Alpha and meant to be paired with Berke. History be damned and end of story.

Finding Gabriella was simply an "in your face" way of being hit with the truth.

Rage pounded at Berke, shoving at his control, and his wolf jumped to the fore, sensing imminent danger. They knew it was Jack, knew that the two of them would be well matched, but it'd end up bloody.

Pushing away from the wall, he turned toward the source of the fury-tinged emotions, intensity growing as Jack closed the distance between them. He tracked the other wolf's progress, noting the disturbances in the crowd while Jack pushed and shoved other Alpha Pairs aside. Growls preceded his friend's advance, snarls joining in with the sounds until it seemed a mass challenge was inevitable.

Aw, shit, the Ruling Alphas really were gonna kick his ass for this. Maybe shoving Jack at Gabriella had been a mistake. Just then his friend burst through the crowd at a run, gaining speed with every step, and Berke spread his legs, waiting for Jack's attack. It wasn't long in coming.

In two massive strides, Jack was upon him, fist colliding with Berke's jaw in an echoing crack of bone against bone.

He stumbled back under the force, shoes sliding over the polished marble floor. Warm wetness coated his chin, and he wiped the throbbing skin. Pulling his fingers from his flesh, he found exactly what he'd been expecting.

18

Blood.

Berke straightened, facing his best friend and Alpha
partner—whether he accepted it or not—and waited for
what came next. He didn't raise his fists to retaliate or allow
his wolf free to tear into the man. No, he stilled and waited.

Jack shook out his hand, redness from the strike already
blooming across his knuckles. "You fucking *dick*."

Another punch came, aimed at his head once again, and
Berke ducked, dodging it easily. All the while, his friend's
emotions pummeled and pounded against him. Anger was
readily recognized, the fury written over Jack's features. But
beneath the rage, hidden under the swirling hints of red and
black that lurked within his best friend, there was pure
unadulterated fear. That stark emotion sent a shiver down
his spine, his body reacting to his partner's feelings.
Adrenaline unrelated to the fight poured into his veins.
Fight-or-flight beat at him, yet the emotion was anchored in
the past, their combined history, and had nothing to do with
today.

"Now, Jack..." The next strike collided with his stomach,
forcing him to double over. Jack took advantage, clipping his
jaw once again.

"You knew, didn't you?" Jack's chest heaved with a
combination of rage and alarm.

"Yeah." Berke blocked his friend's next attack.

"We're not—"

He cut off Jack's words with a hit of his own, fist colliding
with the other wolf's kidneys, first one and then the other.

19

The guy would be pissing blood for a little while. Good thing wolves healed so fast, otherwise it would've been days. "We are. You know it. I know it. The fucking Ruling Alphas know it." He ducked and danced aside. "You just need to accept it, Jack."

"I won't be like him, asshole." Jack spat the word "him", the single syllable a curse. "I won't claim a Marked and do that. I won't…"

A hint of regret tinged his emotions and his feelings intertwined with his friend's. Neither of them wanted to be like *him*. Neither of them wanted to be a mate like *him*. Or lead their Pack like *him*. The ephemeral ghost still lingered and blocked their future after all these years.

"Jack…" Berke glanced at the crowd they'd attracted with their confrontation. Alpha Pairs and Marked alike had formed a circle around them. The wolves' eyes held a glowing blood lust while the females looked on with hints of fear and worry. He sighed and slumped forward, letting his hands rest on his knees while he dropped his head. "It's time, Jack. Now. Today. This second."

The other wolf shook his head, his terror assaulting Berke with every beat of his heart. It pummeled him with its intensity. "I won't do it. Ever. Find some other woman—"

"Don't worry, it's a nonissue now." The voice struck Berke's heart, sinking into his soul like every other word Gabriella had ever spoken. He found her amongst the crowd, bracketed by her livid sisters with the Ruling Alphas standing just behind the three women. "The last thing I want to do is tie myself to two men who don't want me."

With that, Gabriella spun and pushed past her family, shoving aside even the Ruling Alphas in her haste to leave them behind. Her eyes glistened in the light of the hallway, and he fought to deny that they were gathering tears. Pain unlike he'd ever known beat at his heart, threatening to crush him in its intensity. She'd walked away, run, due to Jack's absolute terror of turning into his father.

Berke felt Jack's regret push into him, overtaking the lingering remnants of the man's rage and fear. He swung his attention back to his friend. "Damn it, Jack."

The wolf opened his mouth, but words never came forth.

"You two, with us." Madden, the larger of the Ruling Alphas, broke through the growing tension.

"Now." Keller was smaller yet no less fierce than his partner, and his order brooked no argument.

Straightening, Berke took a step toward the retreating wolves, his training overcoming his dread at what was to come. They'd crushed Gabriella and deserved whatever justice Keller and Madden decreed.

Striding past Jack, he paused at his friend's words. "I'm sorry, Berke. I really am. I never meant—"

He sighed and stared into eyes he knew better than his own. "I know, but apologies and 'never meants' aren't going to do anything to help us when we claim Gabriella." Berke glared at Jack when he opened his mouth to speak. "And we *are* claiming her. Whether she likes it or not." Moving past his best friend, he called to him over his shoulder. "Jack, I suggest you learn how to grovel. I know I will be."

21

CHAPTER TWO

Gabby wasn't going to stop until she got to her sister's penthouse suite. Well, Scarlet was sharing it with her mates and Gabby and Whitney, but she still felt like it wasn't her place. Especially when the Ruling trio got busy, and those moans could be heard in nearly every room. She knew (conceptually, not actually) that sex could be fun-times, but she didn't want to *hear* her sister getting it on.

Ick.

Gabby embraced the silence of the elevator as it ascended, but anger and indignation still thumped through her. She didn't imagine she'd be left alone for long, and her insecurities and humiliation poked and prodded her through the interminable rise.

God, not only did they not want her, the Lieutenant seemed disgusted by the idea of mating her. Oh, he'd growled and done the wolf-y "mine" thing at the table, but the moment his human half regained control he'd run.

A low *ping* announced her arrival, and Gabby slipped through the doors the moment they opened enough for her to pass. She stomped into the suite, ignoring the regular guards stationed throughout the penthouse as she traveled deeper into the space. With every step, she took a breath and released it slowly, fighting to regain her composure before she blew her top.

She hadn't asked to be Marked when she was born. She hadn't asked to come to the Gathering. She hadn't even asked to find her mates. Nope, none of it. But since she hadn't had a choice in the matter, she'd resigned herself to mating two wolves. Two wolves who, by all accounts, would love and cherish and boink her from this day forward 'til death did them part.

She strode into the living room and chose to ignore the sight of her sister's bra tossed over the back of the couch as well as a pair of boxer briefs forgotten beneath one of the club chairs. Apparently Scarlet and her mates had a little fun while Gabby suffered through the Tests of Proximity. The clothing served as a tangible reminder of what Gabby would never have.

She wasn't sure how long she remained locked in her mind, but eventually the soft shuffle combined with wheezing gasps told her that her sisters had finally made it up the stairs. Part of her felt bad that they'd been forced to make their way to the penthouse on foot, but the rest of her was too wracked by anguish to worry for too long.

Huffing out a breath, she spun and faced the crowd that'd followed her. The nearby guards' expressions shifted from piteous to speculative and on to confused. And her sisters, her loving, amazing, best sisters ever, looked ready to go homicidal on someone. Well, someones.

"That happened, right?" She directed the question to the room at large, not expecting an answer. But she had to ask just the same. "I mean, based on his behavior, I'm ninety-nine percent sure the Lieutenant is one of my mates. I figure the Captain is the other, since I got all hot and bothered and my Mark reacted at breakfast. But the whole rejection thing downstairs… That wasn't some nightmare like when I used to dream about going to school naked?" Gabby spun away from the group.

"Um..." Whitney. Poor Whit wasn't big with confrontation.

"I wasn't just embarrassed in front of the *entire fucking Gathering* and rejected by my mates in front of the *entire fucking Gathering* or anything, right?" She took a slow breath. No sense in screaming the roof down. "Because the point of the *entire fucking Gathering* is for wolves to find mates!" So much for not screaming.

"An Alpha Pair rejected you?" There was a tone of utter disbelief in those words, and she swung her attention around to a wide-eyed guard stationed along the wall.

"Ixnay! Ixnay!" Scarlet half-whispered, half-yelled at the guy, but Gabby had already heard him.

"Yes!" She marched up to the wolf in question—whom she decided to call Hello Sexy—and his eyes grew wider with every foot closer she got to him. Cupping her breasts, she jiggled the mounds. "Are my boobs too small? Is that it?" The guard remained silent, and she looked over her shoulder, trying to see her butt. Spinning, she presented him with her backside. "Maybe it's my ass. Is it too small? Or big? I bet we could bounce a quarter off that shit." She wiggled her ass and focused on Scarlet. "Hey, gimme a quarter and give it to tall, furry, and silent here. We're gonna see if it bounces off my ass like peanuts bouncing off of that wrestler's man-titties when he did that pec tightening dance thingy in that movie."

Whitney raised her hand like they were in school. "Pec Pop of Lurve."

"Yes, that's it! We'll call this the 'Butt Bounce of Gabby Getting Rejected in Front of the *Entire Fucking Gathering*'." She forced a grin to her lips, ignoring the thumping pain in her heart.

"Uh, I've got a quarter." The deep, rolling voice coming from the man behind her sank into her bones. Damn, if she hadn't found the two assholes she was meant to be with, she'd throw herself at the altar of Hello Sexy.

She peeked over her shoulder and flashed the guard a smile. "Perfect. Get to bouncing, baby."

A deafening roar, followed by a snarl, echoed off the walls, and she tore her attention from Hello Sexy to the entryway.

"Touch her and die!" The words came from a half-shifted wolf with dark hair. His green eyes sparkled with rage, those orbs the only hint as to the man's identity. His mouth had formed to a wolfen maw, and deep silver fur covered each inch of his exposed body.

"Mine!" Another beast stood beside the first intruder, just as shifted and deadly looking as the other, with dark hazel eyes and amber blanketing him.

Great, it was Tweedle-Find-Some-Other-Woman and Captain-Dick-Head. Obviously they'd escaped the Ruling Alphas.

The two man-beasts came toward her, lumbering steps bringing them closer with every passing heartbeat. She released her breasts, holding her hands out in an effort to halt their approach. Tension, rage, and fury battered at her, the wolves' anger palpable in the room, nearly choking her with its power.

"Nu-uh, furballs. No interrupting the BBGGRFEFG." At
their confused looks, their bushy eyebrows lowering and
wolf lips dropping into a frown, she elaborated. "It's the
'Butt Bounce of Gabby Getting Rejected in Front of the
Entire Fucking Gathering'. You know, because the two of you
rejected me. In front of the *entire fucking gathering.*" Low growls
were their only response, but it was the third throaty sound
behind her that drew her attention back to Hello Sexy.
"Uh…"

"Gabriella, tell the wolf to back off before we do it for him."
Amber guy bared his teeth, snarling in warning.

Lovely.

"Mine!" The silver wolf took a step forward, flexing his
claw-tipped hands.

She reached behind her and patted the guard. She may nearly
hate (okay, dislike a lot) her mates, but she wasn't willing to
risk another's life. She knew how protective and possessive
wolves could be. As evidenced by the fact that Madden and
Keller had killed an Alpha Pair the previous night, when two
idiots threatened both their position and mating to Scarlet.

"I'm good, Hello Sexy." Dear God she did not just say that.
Snarls came from her mates. Okay, she did. "I'll take care of
them. Why don't you run and hide." She kept her gaze
focused on the Captain and Lieutenant, noting the shift of
muscle and bone beneath their skin. "For a while. Years
even."

The guard eased from behind her and edged toward a nearby
hallway. All the while, her mates' gazes remained transfixed
on him. The moment he stepped out of sight, the hostility in

27

the space eased, lowering from Kill Everything to Maim Everyone.

The rapid, heavy thump of booted feet colliding with the marble floors announced newcomers, and Madden and Keller slid into the room directly behind the Captain and Lieutenant. (How fucked was it that she *still* didn't know their names?)

Breathing heavy, Keller bent and propped his hands on his thighs, fighting for air. "They…" He took a deep breath. "They got away."

Scarlet's voice broke into the ensuing silence. "Thank you Captain Obvious." She huffed. "Now gather them up and send them on their way again now that you've caught up with them."

"Scarlet…" Madden had just as much trouble breathing as Keller. "There are things going on that you don't understand. There's some history and magic here that are beyond your compreh—"

"Comprehension?" Scarlet froze and turned toward the Ruling Alphas, eyes blazing.

Gabby kinda wished she had some popcorn now. This show was about to turn *awesome*. Even Whitney, normally quiet and reserved Whitney, snickered and fought against a grin.

"I wouldn't understand?" Scarlet's voice was low and filled with soon-to-be explosive anger.

"Scarlet…" Keller kept his voice soothing and low while glaring at Madden.

Best. Day. Ever. If Gabby's life was going to be filled with drama, it was only right that her sister was there with her.

"Lemme ask you something: I'm the ruler of the vagina, right? Queen of Vaginaville, home of the platinum plated hoo-ha. So, how does it feel to have your passport revoked?" Scarlet flashed the men a smile, exposing all of her teeth.

Even Gabby's half-shifted mates chuckled at that one, earning them a glare from the Ruling Alphas.

"You've got your own problems," Madden snapped.

"Go fix your issues while we deal with this." There was an unmistakable order in Keller's words.

The men moved faster than a blink. One moment the Captain and Lieutenant were on the other side of the room, and the next they were next to Gabby. The Captain swung her into his arms and the Lieutenant leaned toward her, rubbing his fur-coated cheek against hers.

She hated that she responded, that her Mark pulsed in recognition, and her body grew hot and heavy with desire. She wanted them desperately; she just didn't *want* to want them. At all. Hated it even.

Glaring at the men in turn, she didn't bother struggling against the Captain's hold, grudgingly allowing him to carry her off to another section of the suite. As they moved through the space and past her sisters, Scarlet's voice continued to rise.

"Deal with this? *Deal with this*? Oh, there's nothing to *deal* with. Wait, maybe there is. Why don't you *deal with* finding your fucking Wardens and figure out what the hell is going on with Whitney, huh?" With that, Scarlet stomped in the other direction, Whitney laughing and trailing in her wake.

Which left Gabby. Alone. With her mates. At least one of which didn't want her.

*

Jack fought the beast with every step, pushing and shoving at his wolf as they traveled down the hallway. His every inhale brought with it more of his mate's seductive scent. It held those hints of cinnamon and apples and woman that he recalled. Recalled. God damn, it seemed like an eternity between finding Gabby and now.

So much had changed, yet nothing at all. He still didn't believe he should have a mate. Didn't believe he was capable of treating a woman as she deserved. And a mate deserved much.

Yet…yet he couldn't imagine letting her go. Not when she was so close, cuddled in Berke's arms like a babe. She laid her head on his friend's shoulder with a sigh and then those chocolate eyes focused on him, delving into his soul. That sweet contentment that'd been drifting across her features was wiped away by anger, fear, hurt… He'd caused those emotions, been the source of her heartache, and he slumped beneath her gaze. Already he'd chipped away at whatever burgeoning connection they'd made.

Already he was like his father.

Already he'd hurt those he loved. Or, at least, would come to love someday.

How long before he destroyed them all?

Berke's progress slowed, easing as he stepped into a room on the left. The moment he moved across the threshold, Gabby's scent grew, the room holding her flavors. Jack inhaled, drawing the aroma into his lungs, and the wolf reacted, snapping and snarling, urging him to mate with their luscious Gabriella. Now.

A look at the woman in question, her shuttered expression, showed that his desires wouldn't be satisfied any time soon.

With care, the Captain lowered their mate, her body sliding along his front until her feet settled on the floor without a sound. Her eyes were wide, pupils dilated, and a gentle blush stained her cheeks. Then the most delicious scent drifted to him on the barely-there breeze from the air conditioner.

Heavenly musk, hot and thick in the air, hanging heavily as it coated him in the aroma of her essence. Sweet Gabby was aroused, not unaffected by their presence and closeness. His left bicep pulsed and throbbed in recognition while his cock thickened within his uniform pants, filling what little room he had. His prick ached to be free, and damn the consequences.

But he already cared for her, and his emotions weren't enough of an incentive to throw her life away, throw Berke's life away. They could mate, could love, but someday it would all crumble apart into puddles of blood and gore.

Berke's arms remained firm around Gabby's waist, holding her against his body, and Jack couldn't get over how petite the Marked was when cuddled against his friend. He couldn't seem to move past the way her wavy brown hair cascaded over Berke's forearms. Or how her abundant curves molded to the other man's body like a finely-tailored suit. She was meant for Berke. No question about it.

31

Jack could feel Berke's contentment through the half-formed bond that existed between them. It flowed with emotions and arousal. He craved Gabby like a drug, true, but there were deeper, stronger emotions in play. Already the draw of a wolf to a mate laid down the foundations of love.

Unfortunately, Jack felt the same. Fear collided with his soul-deep need, flowing over and through him, shredding the feelings that'd begun blooming. It pounded and pummeled every ounce of caring that her presence had cultivated, and the wolf howled in protest. His beast demanded he surrender to Gabby, follow his instincts and mate the woman before she realized that he wasn't good enough to stand at her side.

Berke leaned down and nuzzled Gabby, burying his now human face in her hair and breathing deep. Those drowsy brown eyes met Berke's for the barest moment, her arousal easily apparent, and then fluttered closed. She moaned and tipped her head back, opening herself to his friend's touch with abandon.

Jack flexed his hands, fighting his wolf with every ounce of his energy, refusing to allow his instincts to lead him on the path to hell. Closing his eyes, he pleaded with the wolf, begging him to recede so that he could stop what was to come. Words were spoken easier through a human mouth rather than a wolfen maw.

Seconds ticked by and his fur slipped back through his pores, the beast allowing him to appear human once again. His face shifted, bones and muscles changing until no hint of his wolf remained in his features.

Unfortunately, his freedom from the beast's control was only on the surface. He took an involuntary step forward, and then another, each shift of muscle pushing him closer to his destined mate. He didn't want this, want her. Not really. She was too beautiful, too innocent to know what mating to him would mean.

Heartache. Pain. Death.

But maybe he could be different than his father… No.

Yet he still moved, boots silent on the thickly carpeted floor. One pace and then another. Another, another, another… Until he stood beside the entwined couple.

Unable to resist the temptation, he slid a single finger along Gabby's cheek. He cataloged the softness of her skin, the increased flush, and the way her breath hitched with his touch.

Low murmurs filled the room, the deep tone of Berke's voice unmistakable, but Jack couldn't force himself to pay attention to his friend's words. He could feel the heat of Gabby's body. The heady scent of her need wrapped around him with ethereal, welcoming arms. Her aroma was like a physical thing, caressing him with invisible strokes and sliding beneath his clothing to pet his skin.

He wanted. God damn, he wanted.

A soft gasp was her only response to his touch and nearness, her eyes fluttering open until their gazes clashed. He watched the expressions that flitted across her features, anger and fury warring with arousal and need. Other emotions clouded her gaze: distrust, attraction, wariness, and then a hint of tenderness and affection that he didn't want to accept. Because he found himself feeling the same.

Jack let his finger slide over her lower lip, noting the difference in texture and softness with his tiny caress. Gabby opened her mouth, and her small, pink tongue darted out to lap as his digit. The warm touch went straight to his dick, forcing him to harden further while his beast howled in triumph. It was cocky and proud, rejoicing in the fact that his human half hadn't destroyed their chance at mating with the luscious creature that called to them.

She did call to him, the siren's song beckoning him closer, inviting him into her seductive world.

The question became: could he ever love her enough not to kill her?

*

Gabby should stop, push the Captain away and punch the Lieutenant in the junk. Yeah, that sounded good. And she'd do that. Just as soon as the Captain stopped laving her neck with his talented tongue, or ceased murmuring a combination of endearments and pleas between whisper-soft kisses.

The gentle words had begun the moment he'd carried her into the room. His low voice delved into her and wrapped around her heart as if he'd belonged there from the beginning of time.

Then again, he had. Both of them were meant to fit and fill her body…someday her heart.

Unable to resist, she lapped at the Lieutenant's finger, allowing his innate flavors to flow over her tongue. Warmth suffused her, sweetness and man filling her mouth with that simple lick. The Captain's words filled her ears while the other wolf's presence crept into her heart.

"Give him a chance, sweetheart..."

"We both want to love you..."

"He's broken, but you can heal him..."

"Don't give up on us before we can prove ourselves to you, love..."

"We'll cherish you..."

"You belong to us... Forever..."

"Our gorgeous, sexy mate..."

Okay, the gorgeous and sexy got to her. Like, really. Her body heated and pussy moistened, not just because of his words, but his nearness and touch as well. Anger was pushed away to make room for arousal. She had no doubt that her rage would rekindle and rush forward the minute their seduction ended, but for now she'd embrace the two men meant for her.

The amber wolf pulled his finger free of her mouth, and she noticed his breathing, the rapid rise and fall of his chest. His eyes glowed yellow in the room's subdued lighting, telling her how close his wolf lurked. He'd shifted like the Captain, assuming his fully human skin once again, revealing his handsome features. She hadn't gotten a good look at the man when he'd first embraced her in the restaurant and then rejected her in the hallway.

Dark red wavy hair framed his face, strands falling across his eyes. The soft threads partially obstructed her view. As she stared at him, those eyes faded from yellow to their natural hazel hue, flecks of green dancing amongst the hints of brown. Like all male wolves he was tall, much taller than her five feet four inches, and muscular with broad shoulders and thick arms. She had no doubt that not an ounce of fat decorated his strong body, a stark contrast to her abundant curves.

She glanced down his body and noted the large bulge at the juncture of his thighs. It appeared the Lieutenant didn't mind her plump body, large breasts, wide hips, and full ass.

She whined when he brought the slick digit to his mouth and slid it between his lips. Heat flared in his gaze, and he leaned closer to her. He released himself with a soft, lingering kiss to the tip of his finger. "Delicious."

"Yes, she is." The rumbled words against her neck reminded her of the Captain's presence, his solid body pressed against her.

The thick length of his hard cock branded her hip, showing her how much he desired her. Did he want her—Gabby—or was he only hard because she was his mate? The same question could be posed to Jack. The amber haired wolf had denied her, but here he stood, hard and seemingly ready to claim her forever.

Her neck was treated to another long lingering kiss followed by a light nibble, a barely-there scrape of the Captain's fangs. Her pussy clenched in response, panties growing damper by the second, and her nipples hardened within her silk bra. The heat, the need, was just as Scarlet had described. Her body called out for both men, the morning's events be damned.

The amber wolf leaned toward her, eyes lightening with every breath. He paused inches from her, motionless and silently asking for permission before moving farther.

She couldn't have held the single word within her had her life depended on it. Arguments could come later. Right now she needed what he offered. "Please."

The Lieutenant struck like a snake, slamming his lips against Gabby's in a fiercely possessive kiss, capturing and holding her tight within his grasp. He forced his way into her mouth, plunging and sweeping into her depths without hesitation. His taste exploded, bathing her with his masculine heat and warm sweetness. She twined her tongue with his, giving and taking in equal measure.

He pressed against her, molding his front to her side, crowding her as the Captain's arms remained around her waist. The heat from their embrace seared her very soul, and she was weak from their dual assaults. Teeth and lips explored her neck while another set ravaged her mouth.

She sucked and flicked the amber wolf's tongue, teasing him and urging his passion higher. Another arm slid around her back, a third joining the Captain's to touch and stroke her. Sexual heat slithered through her veins, sending her blood boiling.

There was no doubt that she wanted these two men, these two wolves, but there were still so many unanswered questions. Her body begged her to relent, sink into them and damn the consequences. Except the rational side of her, the bit that realized that if she gave in right now, knew they'd be tied together with no way to part.

Easing back, she pulled from the kiss, struggling to end the enticing torment of his lips. A second longer and she'd beg them to take her, bite her, and claim her.

With one last burst of self-restraint, she wrenched her mouth from his. There. It was over. His tempting mouth was no longer firm against her lips, and she was able to breathe once again.

Gabby pushed at the wolf holding her, easing him away, and she stepped out of their combined embrace. Growls rolled after her, but she held up her hands, forestalling their approach.

"No." She shook her head. "Fifteen minutes ago you," she looked at the amber wolf, "didn't want me. Five minutes later, you scared another wolf from my side. As far as I know, you aren't even an Alpha Pair. How did this happen?"

Their muscles bunched and tightened, pressing starkly against their tanned skin. She turned to the Captain, admiring his closely cropped black hair and glittering green eyes. Like the Lieutenant he was heavily muscled, tall and filled with barely constrained power. She fought against the need to go to them, mold herself to their bodies and beg for their touch once again. There were too many unanswered questions and too much standing between them. She needed answers before submitting to their claiming.

"Hell, I don't even know your names!"

The two men looked to each other, their gazes communicating something she didn't understand, and then the Captain turned to her, his stare intent. "There are things that need to be said, and we can proceed as you wish."

As she wished.

CHAPTER THREE

As you wish. Uttering those three words took every ounce of Berke's strength. He didn't want to give her a choice, just as he didn't want to give Jack the option of walking away.

"I'm Berke Davis, Captain of the Ruling Alphas' Guard, and this is Jack Wright, my Lieutenant." He took a deep breath, begging his wolf to remain calm. The beast was fighting to break free, dispense with human speech and jump ahead to the claiming. "You are correct that we aren't an Alpha Pair, and yet we are."

Gabriella's brows lowered as her lips puckered in a small frown. His hands tingled with the need to wipe away the expression. Nothing but smiles should ever grace her features.

Reaching for her, he snared her wrist in a gentle hold and tugged her toward a nearby couch. Thank goodness they had somewhere to sit other than the bed. He settled her onto the plush surface, sitting beside her as Jack slumped into a nearby chair. Trepidation poured from his friend in never ending waves. There was no gentle ebb and flow, merely an ever-pounding surf of emotion.

Silence remained heavy, circling them in an undulating current. So many words in the English language, yet he couldn't find a single one.

"Jack?" He looked to his friend, not sure what he was asking, but he asked just the same.

"Yes." Jack nodded, shoulders slumped, and he could feel the heaviness of the other wolf's heart.

Yes to their history then.

Berke twined his fingers with Gabriella's and squeezed her hand gently. He frowned at their conjoined hands, hunting for the place to start their tale.

"The beginning usually works." Her tone was wry, and a glance at her face showed a smirk decorating her lips.

Apparently he'd said his thoughts aloud.

With a sigh, he began...

"Jack and I were born into the same Pack, a small one tucked up in the Georgia Mountains." He let his mind drift to his childhood, remembering the scents of earth and trees, of stone and sunshine on the mountain. "He's the only son of the Alpha trio, and I'm just a regular wolf who happened to be born a bad ass." He puffed out his chest, grinning, and both Gabriella and Jack laughed at that.

"You wish, asshole." His friend snorted.

"When we were kids..." He furrowed his brow, thinking back. "What, we were five? Six?"

Jack shook his head. "Try four. We were precocious, Mom said."

Damn, they'd been younger than he remembered. "We'd been listening to adults talking after the run about how Alpha Pairs were together forever and that they'd never be apart, right?" A sharp, jagged shot of agony pierced him, the emotion assuredly coming from Jack. "We were best friends, *are* best friends, and we didn't want anyone to separate us. We thought if we became an Alpha Pair, they couldn't tell us we couldn't play together."

This time it was Gabriella who snorted.

"Yeah," he smiled ruefully. "Precocious, right? We snuck away that night and crawled into the tree house that we were *definitely* not allowed to be in, and tried not to cry when we…"

"Formed your bond."

Berke shook his head. "A pretty way of saying two four year olds cut open their hands on a rusty nail and pressed our palms together while doing our damnedest not to burst into tears. We were Alphas. Alphas don't cry."

"I wasn't the one crying ya big baby." Jack smiled wide. "You should have seen him, Gabby. Big, bad Berke with tears in his eyes and telling me that we could be Alphas next year when we were 'this many'." His friend held up his hand, fingers spread wide.

Berke snagged a pillow and flung it at the other man. A bit of the pain traveling over their connection lessened and allowed him to take a deep breath. "Ass."

Gabby stroked the back of his hand with her thumb. "So, you two put on your big boy britches and blood bonded."

He nodded. "Yup. Four years old and we'd tied ourselves to each other. Any other boys would have simply gone home with cuts on their hands. Maybe a few bruises."

"But you two are Alphas through and through, so it worked. And it was never finished because…"

There were two stages to becoming a true Alpha Pair. First, they had to live through being bloodied in front of another wolf equal in strength to their own. Had Jack been even a hint weaker than him, Berke would have instinctively taken out the perceived threat to his life. Being injured before another made a wolf jumpy, prone to violence. Because they were evenly matched, their wolves hadn't gone on the offensive, recognizing that a battle between them would only end in pain with no victor. A werewolf version of "you can't kick my ass and I can't kick yours, so let's grab a beer."

So, they'd gotten the hard part out of the way first. Two four-year-old boys who'd decided that they didn't want their moms keeping them from playing together.

Berke opened his mouth to respond to Gabriella's unfinished question, ready to hurry through his explanation as quickly as possible, only it was Jack who stepped into the silence.

"Because one of my fathers murdered my mother and my other dad the day before I turned sixteen." Jack's voice was quiet, but the words sliced through the room. Gut-wrenching heartache shot at Berke from his connection to the other wolf. The feelings nearly had him doubling over in pain. "He said that Berke and I were too strong. He wasn't going to lose his Pack to two snot-nosed teenagers."

Berke replayed the words, the horror of finding one of his Pack's Alphas covered in his mate's blood, grinning and exposing red-hued teeth, and the bodies on the floor barely recognizable. He clenched his fist tight, barely noticing the sting of his nails digging into his palms. It'd hurt him, sure, to lose their leadership like that. But Jack...

"He said the Ruling Alphas could take over for all he cared, but he'd be damned if some other man's whelp would push him out of his place at sixteen." Jack's voice was hoarse and stretched thin.

"But..." Gabriella shook her head, brow furrowed. "But any children in a triad belong to both men. They're—"

Burke tightened his grip, taking comfort in the feel of her skin beneath his. "It was obvious that Jack was genetically Arthur's, and the two of us together were easily stronger than Jack's parents. Even in our teens. So, Walter thought that Jack and I wanted the Pack."

"In his twisted mind..." Jack's eyes drifted closed. The agony was evident, not just in their bond, but also on his features. "There was just so much fear. Fear that the bond would be complete and that we'd suddenly decide we wanted to take over. Everything."

*

Dear God. She'd never heard anything so...heartbreaking. The thoughts of what these two men experienced at sixteen sank into her heart and tore it to pieces.

Squeezing Berke's hand gently, she released him and rose from her seat to go to Jack. She wasn't connected to them as she would be once they mated, but his blazing anguish was easy to see on his features. His eyes glistened, light reflecting off the tears forming. He blinked away the moisture upon her approach, but she'd already caught sight of his vulnerability. And it touched her like nothing before.

43

Berke, with his blatant sexuality and interest, wanted her. There was no doubt. But Jack… He needed her. Berke had been right in that. She could heal him, could show him that being an Alpha didn't mean heartache and loss. It was about love. Love of his Pack, his mate, and any pups that came along the way.

Sliding her hand into Jack's, she forced one arm aside and then slipped onto his lap. He didn't grunt or groan under her plump weight. He simply allowed her do as she wished while she got comfortable. Laying her head on his shoulder, she placed her other palm over his heart.

"It isn't like that. Not truly."

Jack's arms wrapped around her waist, holding her close as he laid his cheek atop her head. "I wish I could believe that. I wish I could go to the Ruling Alphas and complete my bond with Berke and then claim you, Gabby."

Such a stark wistfulness in his voice brought tears to her eyes.

"Jack—"

"No. Even if something like what happened to my parents never occurs again, there are still challenges. Look at yesterday. The Colson Alphas Challenged Keller and Madden for their place *and* Scarlet. They died for their mistake." His voice held a grim tone.

Gabby closed her eyes, remembering the bloody fight. Had it only happened last night? Being Marked meant that she was taught about werewolf life, and she knew that the beasts were an aggressive group. She'd just never been faced with the truth before. And she had to admit that, in part, being an Alpha meant facing challengers to their position.

"So you won't ever claim a mate? Claim me?"

"Gabby…" Jack's heart stuttered beneath her hand, his pulse tripping.

"You can become an Alpha Pair and face the threat of challenges someday, or you can stay in the Ruling Alphas' guards and deal with any threats to Keller and Madden." She pulled away from him, a sob sticking in her throat. She knew he meant every word, knew his resolve to never complete his bond to Berke was rock hard. "Every day you face death, Jack. Every. Day. You just need to accept life."

Rising from his lap, she turned toward Berke. Two steps brought him within reach and she leaned down, brushing her lips across his. Her tears were no longer willing to be held back and cascaded down her cheeks, sliding over her face in thin rivulets. "I'm sorry I'll never get to love you. More than I can ever say, I'm sorry."

With that, she straightened and spun, keeping her gaze averted as she padded to the bedroom door. She didn't look back, unwilling to return to them and beg Jack to reconsider. He'd made his choice long ago. He'd forced back the bone-deep need to complete the bond between him and Berke out of pure fear.

Unfortunately, the prospect of happiness wasn't strong enough to break through that barrier.

Unseeing, she shuffled through the suite, blinking her eyes in an effort to slow her tears. Three steps into the living room, she ran into her sisters, the two of them laughing and chatting as they watched TV. As if sensing her presence, they turned to her, and their smiles slipped from their lips.

"Gabby?" Whitney rose from her seat, concern in both her tone and features. "What..."

"Gabs?" Scarlet popped up and strode toward her, Whitney hot on her heels. "Who do we need to kill? The guys will do that for me. Totally. It's a perk."

Just another reminder that wolves were a bloodthirsty, deadly race.

Gabby shook her head, and when Whitney reached for her, she went willingly into her sister's embrace. "No. It's fine. It is what it is and—"

"What's with the tears?" Scarlet stroked her back, comforting hand tracing her spine.

"We're mates, but we won't be mating. Ever. They," another shake of her head. "They've chosen not to claim me." She closed her eyes and tears still leaked from beneath her lids. She ignored the shocked gasps of not only her sisters, but the guards surrounding them as well.

God, could her embarrassment get any worse?

She practically felt Scarlet's glare around the room. The wolves stationed throughout the room quieted completely until not a sound could be heard. "Come on, Gabs. We'll go chill in my sitting room and order enough chocolate to send us into a diabetic coma."

Scarlet's grin was infectious, forced or not, and Gabby felt herself nodding in response. Chocolate fixed everything. Hopefully, even a broken heart.

Allowing her sisters to lead, Gabby followed, eyes pinned to the ground. She didn't want to see their pity; feeling sorry for herself was enough. In moments, they were ensconced in Scarlet's bedroom and snuggled into a collection of chairs and a couch that mirrored those in Gabby's room.

Slumping onto the couch, she hugged a pillow to her chest and curled into herself. She didn't have any words to express her pain. Nothing. Not a syllable or sound to release the agony in her chest.

She'd be the first to admit that she hadn't been thrilled about having to attend the Gathering. The idea that magic would determine her husbands grated on her, and the fact that the Marked had to follow wolfen law scraped against her nerves. It took seeing Scarlet with her new mates for her to realize that her situation might not be *all* bad. But the moment she spied Berke and briefly met Jack changed all of that.

Gabby glanced around the room, noting the scattered clothes and personal items that decorated the furniture and floor. She wanted this: a messy room that came from three people being so wrapped in each other that everything else fell to the wayside.

But she wouldn't have it, would she?

Scarlet huffed, and Gabby could see the fire kindling in her eyes. "So," she cleared her throat. "Lemme get this straight. They know you're their mate and *don't* want to mate you? I mean, I don't get the whole non-Alpha Pair-slash-Marked mating dealio, but it's there for you three."

47

"Yup." Gabby sighed and laid it all out for her sisters, explaining the situation in broad terms and leaving out what bits and pieces she thought should stay between her, Berke, and Jack.

Silence reigned at the end of her speech, enveloping them in an oppressive blanket until Scarlet shattered it with a few words. "Was Jack dropped on his head as a kid?" She raised her eyebrows. "Really. That wasn't a rhetorical question. Or maybe," Scarlet sat up straighter. "There's a history of Acute Stupidity Disorder in his family tree. I bet if we shake it, it'd pop out." She tilted her head to the side as if pondering the idea. "Do you think they have pills for that?"

Gabby fought against the giggles forming in her chest, pushing them down with all her might, but she wasn't strong enough. First a snort escaped. Then a chuckle. A combination of the two pushed past her lips then. (A snuckle?) And then a full-fledge attack of the laughs hit her.

Whitney soon joined in, her tinkling giggles adding to Gabby's. "At least it's not Erectile Dysfunction. Or is it?" She waved the question away. "If it is, you're better off without 'em. I mean, ED in their thirties? How much use will you get out of them long term? What if they become immune to the little blue pill?" Whitney shuddered. "Can you imagine a life without sausages?"

Gabby threw her head back and laughed. "Sausages? Really? You can call them dicks, hon."

Whitney wrinkled her nose. "That seems so… *So.*"

Scarlet rolled her eyes. "Whatever Whit-prude."

Relaxing into the couch, some of the tension of the morning drained away. God, she loved her sisters. Her annoying, infuriating, loving sisters.

Except… A flash of bright red caught her eye and she narrowed her eyes.

Gabby needed to amend her thought. She loved her sisters except when they stole things. "Scarlet, is that my *Favorite Top of all Time*?"

"Uh, well…" Scarlet cleared her throat. "I think we should focus on Whitney now, don't you? I mean we need to find the Wardens for Whit and figure things out and—" A soft knock interrupted her sister's obvious attempt at changing the subject.

With a glare at Scarlet, she sprung from the couch and stomped to the bundle of red in the middle of the room, snatching it up and shaking it out to get a better look. Yup. Hers. Scarlet normally did *not* wear red. Too many people use to joke about "Scarlet wearing scarlet." Apparently her newfound mates gave her the confidence to bust out with the cherry red.

A low, "saved by the knock" drifted to her, and she glared even harder.

"Bitch." She grumbled and returned to her seat. Hopefully it was the guards with mounds of chocolate-covered heaven for them. Okay, it was for Gabby, she could admit it. Chocolate cured everything. Including heartache over mates who were so frozen by fear that they couldn't see beyond their past and into their future.

A low murmur of voices drifted toward them, but it was Scarlet's screeches that snared Gabby's attention. "Excuse the fuck outta me?"

She let out a relieved sigh. She could definitely go for dealing with someone else's drama right then. Focusing on another wolf would let Gabby wallow in her own chocolate coated misery. Well, as soon as the sugary sweetness got into her grubby hands.

"Tell the two-bit whore that she can fling herself off the building for all I care. Hell, I'll help her. Lemme open a window." Scarlet flung the door open wide, and Gabby caught site of a very uncomfortable looking guard. Her sister nudged the poor guy before her.

"Alpha Mate, please." The wolf held up his hands as if to stop Scarlet, but Gabby knew that wasn't about to work.

"Please my ass. If some butt-sniffing—" A feminine shriek came from the other room, but Scarlet continued. There was no stopping her once she got going. "Slutty, dog-whore, cum bucket who can only get a mate by trying to take someone else's wants to try and come in here…"

Gabby looked at a pale-faced Whitney and lowered her voice to a whisper. "Cum bucket? Someone's been reading some hard core erotica."

Whitney leaned close. "She claims it miraculously appeared on her e-reader."

She snorted. "*Right*. You think some bitch is trying to take Keller and Madden?" She continued with a sing-song voice. "Scarlet's gonna kick the chick's ass. Doo-dah. Doo-dah."

Suddenly the door was flung wide and a woman barreled into the room, pushing past Scarlet and heading straight for her and Whitney. The female's face was contorted, mouth in a half-muzzle and sprinkles of blonde fur coating her skin. The crunch and crack of bones reforming reached Gabby's ears, and more of the change washed over the stranger.

She jumped to her feet, unwilling to meet the psycho sitting down. Who the hell knew what the chick's problem was, but it seemed to have something to do with either her or Whit.

The female stopped in front of her, lips pulled back in a snarl as she bared her fangs. "Gabriella Wickham, I claim right of Mate Challenge."

Well, that answered *that* question.

CHAPTER FOUR

Gabriella's words were merely a distant hum in Berke's mind, swirling around like ghosts but not truly forming into anything he could understand.

"I'm sorry I'll never get to love you."

They'd sat there, watching her walk from the room, their lives, without a look back. But he couldn't blame her. Marked spent their lifetimes waiting for this moment, this second in time when they'd form a triad and live happily ever after. True, it hadn't worked out with Jack's parents, but Berke had been so *sure...*

Like a puppet, Jack had risen and fled the room, and Berke couldn't find it in him to care where the man went. It'd all come crumbling down. He hadn't expected things to bloom into happiness in a blink, but...it was over before it began.

Even his wolf was quiet, not a growl or snarl to be heard, as if it'd given up.

Pain, both physical and emotional, wrapped around his chest, tightening and squeezing until he could hardly breathe or think. He gasped for air, fighting to remain conscious, begging his body not to betray him.

It was over. Truly.

Berke bent over and then crumpled forward onto the carpet. He gagged, bile rising in his throat, and he dashed away the tears in his eyes. He could die now; right now he'd welcome eternal rest. He wanted to be released from a lifetime of suffering. He wouldn't have Gabriella or Jack with him, so what was the point of continuing?

He could go to the forest, shift and let the wolf take over. Eventually a hunter would find him. Yes, that would work. He just needed to resign first.

Pushing to his feet, he stumbled toward the door, ignoring Gabriella's scent as it grasped at him like a physical thing. It clawed at his clothes, holding him tight and threatening to keep him trapped in the room.

No, that couldn't happen.

He broke free of the temptation and stepped into the hallway. Jack's scent drifted to the left, telling Berke the wolf had taken the back stairs that led to their shared suite on the floor below. So he would go right, into the center of the suite. He couldn't be around Jack right now, not with what lingered between them.

The moment he stepped into the central room, low growls assaulted him and battered him from all sides. A quick glance around the space revealed that every guard exposed their fangs to him and their faces were peppered with fur. He could retaliate, censure them for the insubordination. But why bother? He deserved their scorn and more.

He'd… *They'd* hurt Gabriella.

The ding of the elevator announced a new arrival, but Berke couldn't gather the energy to care. At least, not until a guard entered, leading a smiling Hannah toward the Ruling Alphas' bedroom. When the woman caught sight of him her smile turned evil, a glint of hate tainting her eyes along with a flash of victory.

The sound of a scuffle and yells from the suite had him striding forward, but he was quickly cut off by his own subordinates, their eyes glowing yellow. He nearly bared his fangs, his duty burned into his very soul demanding that he respond to the threat to the Alpha Mate.

"Gabriella Wickham, I claim right of Mate Challenge."

Hannah's voice rang high and clear, and another part of Berke shattered, his soul splintering into a thousand pieces.

He had to find Jack. Now.

* * *

Jack settled on the bar stool and leaned his forearms against the shined wood, letting his weight slump forward as his shoulders drooped. He'd left his heart on the penthouse floor, its broken pieces scattered within Gabby's room and blowing through the space.

He'd gotten what he'd wanted, hadn't he? He was still a single wolf and not part of an Alpha Pair. He didn't have to worry about the blood and gore that could come from taking his position. He was alone.

Raising his hand, he caught the bartender's attention and ignored the sway of her hips as she approached. She was probably trying to entice him. Too bad he and his wolf only wanted one woman—ever—and the bartender wasn't her.

"Shot of Johnnie Walker Blue and leave the bottle." He let his gaze turn to the polished wood of the bar top, and he brushed the lingering woman from his mind. Gabby was all he needed, and his wolf agreed. The beast hadn't stopped howling inside his head since Gabby walked away from him and Berke.

God, Berke. He'd never seen or felt so much pain. Jack was used to having a sore heart, but Berke... He could feel the man shattering, and Jack wasn't sure if the other wolf could live through the loss of Gabby.

Jack had forced one foot in front of the other after Gabby left them, only waiting around long enough to confirm that she'd been whisked away by her sisters. Which meant he'd had to listen to the anguish that laced her words. Then he'd faced the countless wolves that served under him growling and snarling as he passed. There were no words said, but their message was clear.

Jack had found his mate, a female that wolves searched for from the moment they came of age, and had rejected her. Bile rose in his throat, burning him from inside out.

A single amber-filled shot glass was placed before him, a bottle filled with the same liquid just beside. Without a glance at the bartender, he grasped the glass and tossed its contents down his throat, not even noticing the burn of the alcohol. He didn't miss a beat as he poured himself another and gave it the same treatment. He prayed he'd be able to drink enough to get drunk and forget for a while. It was unlikely given his werewolf metabolism, but he could hope. Hope for oblivion was all he had left now.

"You need anything else, gorgeous?" The female purred the words, and all it did was infuriate his wolf, sending the beast to the edge of his control.

Growling, he stared at the woman. His eyes stung, fingers ached with his impending change, and he knew his other half was stalking a hairsbreadth beneath the surface.

"No." He barely recognized the word for what it was.

The woman blanched, all color fleeing her face, and she spun to dash away, leaving behind a cloud of fear. Good. Let him wallow in his misery in peace.

Another shot disappeared, the burn barely noticeable now. After the fourth, he abandoned the glass entirely and merely clutched the bottle, taking gulps as he desired. But his wolf burned it all away, leaving him mostly sober and still filled with the misery of losing Gabby.

And Berke.

And his position as Lieutenant.

He couldn't be around his best friend with Gabriella's absence lingering between them. Nor could he continue working alongside the other guards now that they were aware of his cowardice and no longer respected him as a wolf, not to mention a warrior.

Another gulp that his beast treated like water.

Memories flitted through his mind, the bright red blood of his parents overlaying the tear stained face of his mate. One image would ghost past only to be replaced by yet another, his torment continuing with every passing second.

His father's mouth ringed in blood.

The first drop of moisture clinging to Gabby's lashes.

His father's clawed hands coated in gore.

The anguish in her eyes.

His parents' limbs scattered on the floor.

The sobs that coated her words as she said goodbye.

The final goodbye at his parents' graves.

Jack's chest constricted as if a steel band wrapped around him and squeezed. His heart stuttered as his lungs froze when the truth slammed into him like a runaway train.

He'd said goodbye—given up—and abandoned her before he had the opportunity to even *know* her. He'd tossed away love because he was afraid of the pain. Inside he knew that he was a wolf, a deadly beast who lived and died by tooth and claw.

Jack would fucking die, shatter if he ever lost Berke or Gabby. Life wouldn't be worth living without either of them.

A large, heavy body leaned into him, and he turned to face whoever had intruded on his solitude. Roar building in his chest, he snarled at the newcomer but then bit back the sound. "Berke."

His friend snatched the bottle away and sent it sliding down the smooth bar, the glass gliding over the polished surface with ease. "You have a choice, Jack."

He gulped, the alcohol in his stomach threatening to make a return visit. He'd made a decision, of sorts. He recognized what he'd been trying to do. He'd turned into a damned pussy instead of embracing life. Fifteen years of half of a bond with the man beside him and it'd taken a curvy Marked to make him see the truth.

Berke didn't look at him, his gaze distant. "Because of us—"

"Me. Whatever it is, it's because of me."

He nodded. "Because of you, Gabriella is about to face Hannah in a Mate Challenge."

Jack's wolf rushed forward, shoving past his mental walls. The rapid crack and snap of bones came in a blinding rush of burning pain and boiling rage. Hair didn't seep from his pores but burst from his skin. His fingers reshaped to claws in barely a blink and then he was ready to defend his mate. "Mine."

A jolt of anguish and rage shoved its way over the bond he shared with Berke. "And she would have been had it not been for your refusal to complete our Alpha Pairing." Berke took a deep breath and released it slowly. "Hannah obviously heard about Gabriella. And because the she-wolf is a heartless cunt, she decided that she was my mate, not Gabriella. A Marked can't be a single wolf's mate, can she?" A mirthless laugh escaped his lips. "Hannah has taken the stance that Gabriella is encroaching on her territory and making untrue claims."

"We're not an Alpha Pair." Jack couldn't breathe. The walls of the bar were closing in on him, choking him with the truth.

"And that gave the woman an opportunity to make our lives hell and possibly kill our mate in the process." Barely suppressed fury tinged Berke's words.

Thoughts whirled through Jack's mind like a tornado on crack. "We'll do it. Now. Where are Keller and Madden? They can confirm our pairing, and we'll find a Pack or start our own and we can—"

"Do nothing because the Mate Challenge has been announced and accepted." Berke's grim resignation slid into Jack.

"When?" He choked on the word, his wolfen maw fighting to push it past his lips.

"Now."

* * *

"Now?" Gabby screeched. "Right now? As in this second?" She gulped. Okay, she could do this. Really. And live. Maybe...-ish.

Scarlet was ranting at her mates, the Ruling Alphas. "Go get them right this minute and work your mumbo jumbo and then the fuckdicious assholes can claim her already! What good is it to have the biggest dicks in the room if you can't swing 'em around?"

The two men winced, but it was Keller who spoke. "Now, sweetheart..."

"Don't you 'sweetheart' me. My sister is about to be torn into dog kibble because two of your wolves are pussies." Then Scarlet meowed.

Gabby would have been offended if her sister hadn't been telling the truth. "Has anyone else noticed that she's a wolf, and I'm, I don't know, *human*?"

Whitney stood and glared at the Ruling Alphas. Since she didn't have a Mark and was at the Gathering due to some magical clerical mistake, she had a little more leeway. "What do your stupid furball laws say about *that*?"

Go Team Whitney.

"Actually," a rolling, baritone sliced into their argument. "They say that a Challenge between a wolf and a human shall be conducted in human form. Any hint of the wolf's control slipping results in an automatic forfeit and dismissal of the Challenge."

Everyone's attention shifted to the newcomer. Make that, newcomer*s*. Two wolves stood before them. They appeared to be like any other wolf in attendance, but they held a hint of something *other*.

From the corner of her eye, Gabby watched Whitney sway, body leaning forward and toward the two men as if drawn by a string. Nudging her sister, she burst into the silence.

"And you are?" Gabby raised a single brow.

"The Ruling Wardens. Emmett," he gestured to himself. "And Levy."

"Well it fucking took you long enough." Scarlet's words echoed in the now crowded room.

"It took what it took, Alpha Mate." A smile teased Emmett's lips, and Whitney stepped toward him.

Oh, she didn't like this guy already. Elbowing Whitney once again, she forced her mind back to the issue at hand.

61

"So, no claws or fangs or fur? Just fists and feet?" Scenarios and 'what ifs' tumbled through her mind.

Levy nodded. "Correct."

"How do you determine the winner?" This was the worrisome part. Was it, like, death? 'Cause that would suck.

"First blood." Emmett's voice was flat and matter of fact.

Gabby huffed. Okay, not horrible. Sure, Hannah the Whore was probably faster and stronger than her... And probably had a lot more experience in fighting. But Gabby could pull it off...-ish.

"Okay. First blood. Sticking to skin. I can do it." Gabby nodded, trying to convince herself more than everyone else. "What happens to the loser?"

She wasn't sure she wanted to know, but she needed to ask the question.

"She will be set aside while the winner is given the opportunity to mate with the male in question. The loser will be denied the male."

"So, if I lose, whether Berke wants her or not, she gets a crack at him, and I have to steer clear forever."

"Gabby, no." Scarlet shook her head and glared at her mates. "This isn't happening. You two make the laws." She snapped her fingers at Keller and Madden. "Get to rewriting. You've got some super-magical pen hanging around, right?" She growled. "Give it to me and *I'll* redo the fucking things. 'Cause this," Scarlet waved at Gabby. "So ain't happening."

"Alpha Mate," Levy drew everyone's attention. "The laws are as they have been for centuries. They are what keeps us civilized."

"Civilized?" Contempt coated Whitney's words. "Two assholes fighting Keller and Madden last night for their position *and* Scarlet is considered civilized? And this? Gabby getting Challenged as Berke's mate is civilized?"

"Hannah is claiming that Gabriella is lying and trying to turn her mate against her." Emmett calmly stated the facts.

"And I claim she's a manipulative beyotch. Amazing how anyone can claim anything, innit?" Whitney's voice held scorn, but Gabby could see a hint of something else when she looked at the two Wardens.

God help her. Whitney couldn't be attracted to the two emotionless wolves. Whit most assuredly couldn't imagine having some sort of relationship with them, could she? Because that's what Gabby was seeing. Whit had that dreamy "love me" look, and she knew from experience that it never ended well.

"Whitney," Levy eased into the conversation.

"Miss Wickham." Whitney snapped.

"Miss Wickham," Levy continued. "All Marked are subject to wolf laws and they state—"

Gabby threw her hands in the air. "Do you two know anything other than 'suck it up buttercup'?"

That got her two snickers (from her sisters) and four identical looks of confusion (from the wolves). Apparently furballs didn't grasp everything. Look at how dumb the smart people were.

"Okay, so it boils down to me stepping into the ring with Hannah and fighting for two wolves who *don't even want me.* That's it, right?" The meaning behind the words pierced her heart, nearly bringing her to her knees.

"Unfortunately, their decision to claim you, or not, is not in question. The belief of your status as mates is. Is Berke Davis your mate?" Emmett's gaze was focused on her.

"Yes."

Levy nodded. "Then we should go to the grand ballroom and complete the Challenge."

It was so easily said, yet Gabby struggled to make her feet move. A single word pounded through her mind: blood. Six letters, a single object. So infinitesimal when compared to the entire body. A single cell would end it all.

The thought carried her to the elevator and down to the lobby. It pushed one foot in front of the other as she navigated the hotel's hallways and into the grand ballroom. It nudged her to the edge of the forming circle, and she stared at the evil she-bitch across the rapidly emptying area.

The heavy thud of feet rose above the low murmur of voices, and the crowd parted in a rapid wave. In moments, two men burst into the center of the cleared circle, both of them breathing heavy with exertion. Berke and Jack.

"Stop!" Jack's voice cut into the sudden silence. "Call off the challenge. Gabby belongs to us and—"

Emmett strode toward her mates, well ex-almost-mates. "And are you now a complete Alpha Pair eligible to recognize and claim their Marked."

Jack paled while rage coated Berke's features. "We can do that now. Ruling Alphas please—"

Levy held up a hand and silenced Jack. "Regardless of your status, the Mate Challenge has been issued and accepted. If you'd still like to receive the Ruling Alphas' blessing, you may. However, it won't change what is to happen."

She really, really hated the Wardens. Hated. She wanted someone to pee in their corn flakes and throw a flaming shit bomb at their front door.

Both men swayed, their stricken gazes locking onto hers. They strode toward her, concern and worry in every line of their bodies.

"Gabby..." Jack reached for her hand.

"Gabriella..." Berke grasped the other. "You can't do this. We won't let you."

Gabby shook her head and tugged free of their hold. "It's done. You acknowledged our status as mates, but never formed your Pair and claimed me."

"It wasn't you, love." Jack sounded so sincere.

"Right."

"We're going to ask the Ruling Alphas for their blessing. We want you. I was..." Jack's words trailed off, and Gabby filled in the blanks.

"An asshole? A jerk of massive proportions? A heartless bastard? A pussy?" That'd been her favorite word tossed around today.

"All of the above." He gave her a sad grin.

"Gabriella, I don't..." Berke seemed at a loss for words.

"It doesn't matter." She sighed and shrugged. "I'll be fine. I mean, I know Tae Bo and Turbo Jam, right?" She forced a chuckle. "And, hey, X me baby." She raised her arms and crossed her forearms to make an "X".

Jack raised a single brow in question.

"What? You guys haven't heard of P90X? It's like, the most bad ass workout system ever. I mean, I barely made it through the warm-up, but I totally watched what they were doing." Gabby cracked her neck. "I got this." She turned toward the men who may or may not become her mates. "The question is: once I win, what happens?"

Jack licked his lips, reminding her of what they shared, and lost, not long ago. "With Keller and Madden's blessing, we'll complete our bond and then claim you as ours." He cupped her face and stroked her cheek with his thumb. "There's a lot to say, but I know what I did wrong, and I'll fix it as soon as you take care of Hannah."

Right. The she-bitch.

Berke twined his fingers with hers, tugging her attention from Jack. "She doesn't have any experience in fighting and will probably come at you like a girl."

"Hey, I'm a girl." She narrowed her eyes, and Berke rolled his.

"She won't have any form. Imagine random punches, scratching, and hair pulling. Keep out of her way and try to scratch her first." Berke huffed and Jack picked up on tossing out tips.

"She'll come at you with her nails, but duck and punch her in the stomach."

"Like this?" Gabby made a fist, and Jack shook his head.

"No, like this. Don't cover your thumb. You'll break it." Jack repositioned her fingers and she tried to remember how they were arranged.

"She'll tell you where she's going with her eyes. Wait for it. After the stomach, aim for her face. Nose or mouth will bleed the quickest if you hit 'em." Berke's voice was low and soothing.

"If you can't hit her right off, trip her. Then you can kick her in the face." Gabby opened her mouth to protest, but Jack cut her off. "She's a wolf. She'll heal fast. Your job is to get her to bleed. Don't for a second think she wouldn't do the same to you."

The silence stretched, and Berke looked to Jack, the two of them communicating without words, before turning back to her. "We'll go Rogue before we lose you, Gabriella."

She shook her head, unwilling to accept Berke's solution.

Jack butt in. "Yes. It's decided."

"Jack…" She turned to her previously reticent mate.

"If you'll have us, you're ours. Period. The only thing this spectacle does is delay our mating." Truth rang in Jack's words, each one imbued with sincerity that flowed from his heart.

Scarlet poked her head into their small circle. "But it would be super awesome if you, like, won and shit since Keller found you a kick ass Pack to lead and everything. Just sayin'." Message delivered, she retreated just as quickly as she'd appeared.

"Miss Wickham?" Levy's voice drifted through the growing din.

Straightening her shoulders, she pushed to her tip toes and brushed a kiss across Jack and then Berke's lips. "Lemme go kick this bitch's ass and then we can do the Alpha Pairing mumbo jumbo stuff."

Before she could deal with any more mushy whiny-ness, she strode toward the waiting Wardens. Just as soon as all this was handled, she was so gonna kick their asses for taking so long to arrive and help with Whitney. Maybe she could do the whole Challenge Without Death thing to them once she was done with Hannah.

Right.

Standing in the center of the cleared area, she faced off against the she-wolf, noting the smug look and cocky attitude she displayed. Like Berke was hers already, and this farce was simply a formality. As if.

Levy stood to Gabby's left, body centered between her and Hoe Bag. "Hannah Cox…"

Gabby snickered, earning her a glare from Levy. Whatever.

"…has issued a Mate Challenge to Gabriella Wickham for mating rights to Berke Davis. The fight is to first blood. Ladies, are you ready?"

Could she say no? A glance at Emmett revealed his equally stern glare. Okay, apparently not. "Of course."

This time it was Hannah who snickered, and she added an eye roll for good measure. "Yeah, yeah. Let's do this."

"Show some respect," Levy snapped, exposing the first true flash of emotion she'd seen. Glaring didn't count. She took that as a silent warning. Him biting off Hannah's head, however, was freakin' awesome.

With those last words, he stepped back until he was even with the bodies encircling them. "Begin."

Hannah gave her a smarmy smile, feet moving across the floor as the wolf began circling Gabby. "Ready to lose your 'mate', human?"

Rolling her eyes, she stepped back and countered the wolf's travels, not allowing the woman to get close.

"To a she-whore like you? As if." Gabby kept her gaze intent, looking for any hint of an attack. She wasn't stupid enough to take on the woman first. Nope, she hoped Hannah would leave her with an opening so she could react and win. Berke and Jack had both given her tips on how to defeat the wolf.

So, yeah, watch her eyes, punch her in the stomach, punch her in the face (but no covering her thumb) and pray she bleeds. She totally had this. Maybe...-ish.

"I'm stronger than you, human. Do you really think you have a chance? One hit and Berke will be mine." Hannah's grin was filled with pure evil. "Give up now before you get hurt."

Gabby circled right, allowing the wolf to continue her smack talking.

"We don't want to hurt your pretty face while you're still looking for your mate, do we? Stop this, human." Hannah sneered.

"You know, cunt," Normally Gabby wasn't with using that word when applied to a woman, but it just *fit*. "I think thou doth protest too much." She tilted her head to the side. "Actually, I'm pretty sure you and your little puppy inside are afraid of me. Is that it?" Gabby smirked. "The big, bad wolf is afraid of a little 'ole human."

The wolf scoffed. "Never."

"Really?" Please, please, please let the whore be gullible. "Prove it. Gimme first shot, bitch. A little human can't hurt the big bad wolf, can she?"

Hannah's eyes lightened but didn't flip to the full yellow of her wolf. Damn it. That would have ended this stupid game.

Grumbles and snorts furthered Gabby's case, the gathered crowd obviously agreeing with her taunts. No human could ever hurt a furball; they're too big and growly and strong and blah, blah, blah.

"Fine," Hannah bit off the word and moved to the center of the circle, stilling once she reached her chosen spot. "Do your worst, human. But know that the moment you finish, I'll be doing the same."

Gabby straightened and grinned at her mates. "Dudes, it's like Christmas!"

Turning her attention back to Hannah, she circled the woman, drawing out the suspense. Because, hey, embarrassing the wolf couldn't ever be rushed. She kept her steps slow and steady, already scrolling through her not-so-vast catalog of moves. Tae Bo had punches and kicks and P90X was big on cross-training. But Turbo Jam…

Hello assious kickious.

Stopping before Hannah, facing the woman one-on-one, she smiled wide. "Ready? 'Cause this is gonna be over fast."

Another eye roll from the she-wolf.

Gabby shrugged. "Okay." Getting into position, she raised her fists, Jack's voice practically purring through her mind. Then she kicked ass and told names to fuck the fuck off.

Gabby sped through the moves, the background music from her favorite Turbo Jam video filling her head. *Jab. Cross. Hook. Upper cut.*

Boo-yeah mother fuckers!

A stunned silence wrapped around not only Hannah, but the crowd as well, as if they all held their breath.

Then pain overwhelmed her and she clutched her hand, knuckles throbbing and hurt pounded through her body. "Shit, that fucking hurt. Why did no one tell me it'd fucking hurt?" She screamed the question as she worked through the agony.

She definitely would have remembered a "Hey, it'll feel like you're dying" warning. But even through the pain, she kept her gaze intent on Hannah. 'Cause, yeah, she had no doubt that blood was freakin' inevitable. If punching the beyotch's face hurt Gabby, it had to have hurt the other woman.

Tick tock, Mr. Blood. Any time now.

Only, shit on a stick, the red stuff didn't show. Nope, the she-wolf simply stood in the middle of the circle rubbing her jaw, fingers sliding over slightly reddened skin, and then even that flush disappeared.

An evil grin formed on Hannah's mouth. "My turn." Without pause, the woman struck out at Gabby, her human fingers curved and aimed right for Gabby's face.

Eyes wide, she did the only defensive maneuver she had in her vast arsenal… Okay, she had no arsenal. She did have… *Stop, drop, and roll!*

Gabby hit the ground with a scream and then rolled across the circle before popping to her feet. Oh shit. Shit. She was gonna die and she'd never be with Berke and Jack again. She readily admitted that the worry over dying trumped hot sex with her two wolves. Her wolves. She needed to remember that. She was doing this so she could have them, and no wolf was gonna take that from her.

Hannah came after her again, fingers still curved into human claws, and her mouth was wide, baring her blunted teeth. When the chick was within arm's reach, Gabby dropped again, this time crawling between the woman's legs and dashing to the other side of the circle.

Yes, she was a pussy with a capital Save Me Now.

"Come on, Gabby! Punch her in the junk!" Scarlet's yells rose above the general shouts.

"Junk?" Then Gabby screamed like a girl because Hannah lunged for her. Waving her hands, she ran around the edge of the circle, the wolf hot on her tail. "Do girls really *have* junk?"

Snarls followed her, the other woman closing the gap between them.

She really should have actually *done* the P90X videos instead of just watching them for the man candy. Really.

Suddenly her fleeing was cut off. Hannah managed to snare a clump of Gabby's hair, pulling her up short. She fell backwards with a scream, hitting the thinly carpeted floor with a grunt, and her breath was knocked from her lungs.

Hannah yanked on her hair again, holding Gabby steady as the she-wolf straddled her stomach. Wrenching her head back, the woman leaned toward her.

God, this was it. A single, crushing bite and Gabby would lose her men forever. There'd be no chance of mating if the stupid bitch spilled her blood. The nearer Hannah came to her neck, the quicker Gabby's vision of her future deteriorated. Anguish overtook her, squeezing her heart in an iron grip. Tears sprung to her eyes, not from Hannah's actions, but at the thought of never having Berke and Jack.

Hannah bared her blunted, human teeth. With each inch closer, Gabby fought harder. She struggled against the woman's hold, but her strength didn't allow Gabby to move an inch.

Hanna's face became Gabby's world, the screams and shouts of the crowd drowned out by the terror that coursed through her. Between one breath and the next, she felt more of her future draining away. With luck, the wolf's bite would kill her. She couldn't imagine living without those two wolves.

The she-wolf yanked on her hair again, forcing her head to turn even further, and then Berke and Jack were within sight.

"See them, human? Before you draw your next breath, Berke will be mine. Remember that as your blood flows." Hannah was so smug.

Anger. Fucking rage hotter than anything Gabby had ever felt before pounded through her. No. She wasn't gonna let this happen. Period. Full stop. She dug deep within her, searching out any unused strength, and drew on the last few bits that lingered. Uncaring of any further pain, she turned her head, straining against Hannah's hold, and uttered two, last words. "Fuck. You."

Before the last syllable left her, she'd opened her mouth wide and did what she should have done forever ago. If it was good for the wolves, it was good for humans. In a blink, her teeth met flesh and in a fraction of a second, her jaw clamped down on Hannah's cheek. Blood, coppery and salty, filled her mouth, and the urge to vomit nearly overwhelmed her. Bile rose in the back of her throat and she released the wolf the moment the fluid poured over her tongue.

Screams and yells echoed around her, Hannah's screeches overwhelming them all. The weight of the she-wolf disappeared and Gabby opened eyes she hadn't realized she'd closed.

A strong arm around Hannah's waist kept the woman from coming back at her. The she-wolf's eyes yellowed and fangs burst from her gums as her fingers finally did transform into deadly, claw tipped paws. Blood continued to flow down the woman's mangled cheek, and Gabby almost felt bad for the screeching chick.

Almost.

Okay, not really.

"That's enough, Hannah." Levy's beefy arm held the woman still. "The Wardens' official ruling is for Gabriella Wickham. Hannah Cox will no longer be permitted to approach Berke Davis."

"Bitch," Hannah spat. "I issue a Mate Challenge to Gabriella Wickham for—"

Levy slapped a hand over the bitch's mouth. "No, you really don't."

Hannah shot daggers at Gabby with her eyes.

"The next order of business is the Alpha Bonding of Berke Davis and Jack Wright." Emmett drew her attention, and she noticed the man's focus was on her two mates as well as

Keller and Madden. "Ruling Alphas, do you agree that these two males are worthy of the pairing and give your blessing?"

Keller's answer was immediate. "We do. Gentlemen." He beckoned her mates to the center of the circle, and they both kneeled. Placing his hands on their bowed heads, he spoke the necessary words. "Blood ties to heart. Heart ties to body. Body ties to soul." A soft glow flowed over Berke and Jack. "Heart. Body. Soul. May you rule with your heart, protect with your body, and find the one to complete your soul." The low light flared bright, nearly blinding her with its intensity. "I present the Gathering with Alpha Pair Berke Davis and Jack Wright, the new Colson Alphas."

Colson. Madden and Keller had killed that Pack's Alphas just the previous night. Now Berke and Jack would be taking over. Would the wolves resent them? Hold the deaths of their Alphas against them? Would they...

Scarlet's low whisper broke into her worries. "It's like, fifteen minutes from the Ruling Alpha compound. Sweet, eh?"

"What?" She whispered back, watching her men receive congratulations from the crowd.

"Yeah, Keller and Madden said Colson is close to our home. So you can totally come by for coffee and stuff." A glance at Scarlet revealed her wide smile.

"But if your guys are close, why don't they rule over that city?"

Whit popped into the conversation. "They're responsible for the entire continent. No way they're gonna deal with a small city." Her sister's gaze was intent. "And I know you're

76

worried about the Pack accepting you guys, but everyone said those guys were assholes."

"They didn't break any laws..." Scarlet began.

Whitney finished. "...but they were dicks. So your new gang will welcome you three."

"Three?" She squeaked. Conceptually, she realized that she was Berke and Jack's mate. But reality was slamming into her with a ginormous hammer.

"Three." Scarlet nodded. "They're an Alpha Pair, you're a Marked, and now it's time to boink like werebunnies on crack."

"Do you think there are werebunn—" Gabby didn't get a chance to finish the word. Berke and Jack swooped in then, wrapping their arms around her and turning her toward the exits. Hell, she didn't even say goodbye to anyone. They did that for her.

"It's time to mate, Mate." Berke's voice was filled with sexual promise, but she noticed that Jack hadn't said a word.

"Jack?"

Jack stopped, disregarding the flowing mass of bodies that slid around them. They created their own bubble in the chaos after the Challenge. He released her hand and cupped her face, both palms warm against her cheeks. "I want nothing more than to mate you, Gabby. I made a mistake in not bonding with Berke, and I refuse to repeat it by not mating you. The three of us belong together. My body, my wolf, knew it. It just took some time for my heart to accept the truth as well." He brushed a gentle, chaste kiss across her lips. "You're the one, Gabby. Our Marked. Our Mate."

The truth didn't slither into her veins, but pummeled her chest with never-ending strikes. She fought against the tears gathering in her eyes. "Berke?"

He stroked her back, fingers tracing her spine. "From the moment I saw you, Gabriella. You know that. Our Marked. Our Mate."

She nearly buckled under the weight of their conviction, their assurances flowing over her like water. "Okay. Your Marked. Your Mate." She licked her lips. "Take me to your room and claim me."

"Not the penthouse?"

She wrinkled her nose. "I refuse to boink in the same suite as my sister. It's...icky."

CHAPTER FIVE

Another consciousness lingered at the back of Berke's mind. It drifted, thoughts of its own meandering within him.

Jack.

Formerly blunted emotions coated his own. Hints of fear overlaid with elation were present, and they could only be attributed to his newly acquired Alpha Pair status. There were well and truly tied together now, nothing able to tear them apart save death. His wolf howled with joy, reveling in the presence of the other beast. They had their other half, and it was time for them to claim the missing part of their soul.

Berke and Jack bracketed Gabriella as they rode in the elevator, soft dings announcing each floor they passed. They weren't on the top floor like Keller, Madden and Scarlet, but occupied the level beneath them in the event that they were needed. They even had an inner stairwell that connected the two suites for quick access.

Since they'd probably be claiming Gabriella this night, he prayed it wouldn't be used any time soon. Like, for the next fifty years or so.

One last chime announced their arrival, and the shining metal doors swooshed open to reveal a deserted hallway. With Jack leading the way, Berke allowed Gabriella to precede him while he covered the rear. Ever the warrior, he and his wolf were intent on protecting their backs. It wasn't so much the threat of others as it was his fear of anything ever happening to their mate that urged him to take the stance.

Besides, it gave him the perfect opportunity to ogle her rounded ass. Her rear mounds were plump and full, hips swaying and butt jiggling with every step. He couldn't wait to nibble and nip her flesh, watch the flush of her skin as blood accentuated his bites. He'd leave love marks all over her body, ensuring that everyone knew she was a taken female.

Our female. The voice was soft, his connection to Jack too new for his friend's voice to boom through his mind, but he received it none the less.

Berke followed the magical thread between them, tracing the golden, twining strands until he was met with Jack's consciousness and he projected into his friend's mind. *Our mate.*

He sensed the other man's wolf howl in triumph and agreement. Yes, they were both on the same page when it came to their luscious Marked.

They paused just outside their door, and Jack was quick to gain access to their suite. When Gabriella moved to follow the other wolf, Berke stayed her with a gentle touch to her arm. "One moment, mate."

She frowned at his light restraint, but grinned when the word "mate" left his lips. "Mate…" She whispered.

"Mate." He couldn't withhold the pleasure that the word caused him. "Jack just needs to ensure we're alone before we enter."

Her frown returned. "Why?"

"We were already a target due to our ranks, but we're an Alpha Pair now. We can never be too careful. Especially when it comes to your safety. Regardless of your new status, your body is still human and vulnerable." They would always take care with her. Nothing would ever mar her perfect skin. Not even a paper cut.

Before she could respond, Jack appeared, a hesitant smile in place. "All clear." His unease was nearly palpable, and he reached out slowly to twine his fingers with Gabriella's. "Come in?"

Relief, both his and Jack's, whooshed through Berke when she nodded and stepped into their home away from home. One step became two became a few until they stood in the small sitting area. A subtle shudder wracked her body, and Berke was quick to move toward her, mirror Jack's grip on her opposite wrist and lean into her. Gabriella's curves welcomed him, her body seeming to recognize him with ease.

"We don't have to do this if you're not ready, Gabriella," he soothed as best he could.

We don't? Jack growled, and Berke narrowed his eyes.

No, we don't. Are you forgetting you were an ass mere hours ago? You rejected her, Jack. She's been through a Challenge to keep us, but that doesn't mean she's ready to mate us with abandon. Berke didn't bother keeping the annoyance out of his tone, even adding to the words by sending his emotions along their link.

An immediate flow of contriteness was returned. "He's right, Gabby. We're on your schedule." Jack cupped her cheek, and Berke could feel the sizzling connection. There was attraction and need bouncing between them, but they couldn't forget how they'd hurt her. "When you're ready and not a moment before."

But I can't wait for her to agree. Jack's mental words were a growl more than anything.

I know. Though, if she agrees, I'm not sure how to go about this.

Jack came back sounding so smug. *What? Afraid of sex, pretty boy?*

He wanted to punch his Alpha partner. *So you've been in a threesome? Claimed a mate before? Really?*

A wall of doubt and frustration hit him in response.

Gabriella squeezed Berke's hand but didn't tear her gaze from Jack. "What's with the sudden change of heart?"

Jack froze, tension overtaking his body, and Berke stepped in for his Alpha partner. "Life, no matter the heartache it brings, is always worth living. We wouldn't be living if you weren't with us."

"Jack?" His mate pressed.

His friend's shoulders slumped, and he leaned forward, pressing his forehead to Gabriella's. Berke stroked his mate's back and placed a hand on Jack's shoulder, giving them both support as they crawled over what he suspected was the last hurdle.

"Fear…" Jack's eyes closed. Berke sensed every emotion rolling through his friend. He welcomed them with open arms, taking them into himself in a way he never had before. Jack continued. "Fear of what may be isn't worth losing you, Gabby. I'm an idiot and an asshole for pushing you away, but never again."

The last three words came on a whisper, but based on Gabriella's gusty sigh, she'd heard him clearly. When she slumped into the other man, Berke realized she'd accepted Jack's words. Examining them through their bond, he also recognized them as truth.

Gabriella swallowed, the lines of her neck rippling with the effort, and she cleared her throat. "Okay."

"Okay..." Berke murmured.

"Okay, I want to be yours." Her voice shook.

"You'll never regret your choice, Gabby. We'll spend the rest of our days loving you." Jack's words cut through Berke, slicing through his body and straight to his heart.

Love? So quick? No. It couldn't be... He internally shook his head. No way.

You're telling me you weren't half in love with her the moment you felt her Mark burn on your skin? You know it flickered. Even I felt it and I was fighting this tooth and claw.

Berke refused to accept his partner's words. *No. It can't be—*

It can and is, friend. She was made for us, and I for one am not going to allow fear to stop my heart. I recommend you do the same.

He took a deep breath, stared at the two he'd spend the rest of his life with, and let his bottled feelings fly free. It wasn't a bone-deep, soul-connecting love. Yet. But he had no doubt that, with nurturing, it'd blossom into a tie that could never be broken.

Berke placed a finger against her chin and directed her attention to him. "Gabriella?"

"Make me yours, Berke."

Oh, shit. How the hell are we gonna do this? Berke mentally gulped.

I saw it in a porn once? They were all on their sides and she was in the middle... Jack sounded so hopeful.

We're not taking our mate like porn stars. Berke nearly growled aloud.

Why not? It obviously works. Jack paused for a moment. *I think I could've been a porn star...*

God, he and Jack were in so much trouble. *Let's hope we don't fuck this up... And keep your dick to yourself.*

*

Berke tugged her, drawing Gabby toward an open set of double doors that revealed a massive bed in the center. It was more than enough space for the three of them to come together. Logistically she knew what was to come, but had never actually made love with two men at once.

They would join as one, both of her holes filled with them as they fought for release within her. The final step would come when they sank their partially shifted teeth into her shoulders. One on the left, another on the right. Scarlet had warned her of what was to come, words interspersed with giggles and blushes, but description and reality seemed nowhere near one another.

Their travels stilled at the foot of the bed, the two men bracketing her, settling her between them. Berke remained at her back while the previously reticent Jack pressed against her front. The heat of their bodies crept into and seared her.

Gentle hands stroked her arms, skimming her skin as they sought their way beneath her clothes. Silently, gently, they disappeared. The men worked as one, divesting her of her shirt, then shoes, and finally shorts until she stood before them in nothing but her bra and panties. She was exposed, barely anything left to the imagination. Quiet reigned and unease slithered through her, self-doubt and insecurity creeping to the fore.

For, like, all of a second.

A glance at Jack's features revealed his desire, the tautness of his face and the sharpening of his cheeks and jaw showing her he was close to losing control. His eyes transitioned to a pale yellow that darkened by the second as his wolf peeked at her.

Berke encircled her with his arms, movements stilling as he reached her rounded stomach. "So sweet and soft." A growl shaded his voice.

Palms slid over her skin, Berke's fingers tracing the waist of her panties, digits dipping beneath the elastic. Then he continued farther south until he rested just above her mound.

Oh, God. She ached. Her core pulsed and clit twitched with the need for these two wolves. Arousal thrummed in her veins as her pussy grew heavy and filled with unsatisfied desire. A deep inhale from Jack told her that he'd caught the scent of her need. Her musk permeated the air, and those eyes flashed to the pure yellow of his wolf.

Jack's palms cupped her large breasts, her flesh overflowing his hands, and he squeezed. Her nipples hardened, and he traced the nubs, silk and lace the only things separating them.

"See how she needs, Berke?" Jack murmured, his gaze centered on her chest. She shivered beneath his regard. "So responsive."

While she remained focused on Jack, Berke's fingers danced past her cropped curls and farther south to her soaked pussy. His digits slid through her cream, teasing her slit and then delving into her moist depths. One finger traced her inner sex lips, pad stroking her from hole to clit and back again. The first brush of the sensitive bundle of nerves nearly brought her to her knees.

"Berke!"

"So, very, very responsive. I'd say we're lucky wolves, wouldn't you, Jack?" Berke scratched her neck with a sharp fang.

Another stroke, finger sinking into her sheath and then retreating to her clit. He circled the nub, round and round, and she rocked her hips in time with his ministrations.

But Jack hadn't been a lazy boy. While Berke tormented her pussy, Jack tugged the cups of her bra down to expose her tender breasts. Now there was nothing between his skin and her flesh. He cupped her mounds as if weighing them, teasing her once again until he captured one nub, and then the other, between thumb and forefinger. He plucked and pinched her nipples, his torment adding to the blissful arousal that Berke stoked.

Berke continued his teasing caresses, urging her closer to release. Two fingers replaced one, both sinking into her hole and stretching her. She rocked into his penetration, fighting for him to slide deeper. A sting accompanied his invasion, but it merely added to her arousal.

"Need to get this wet hole ready for us." He laved her neck and suckled her flesh. "I can't wait to fuck you hard and deep. Do you want that sweet Gabriella?" Berke's words shoved her toward the edge, and an uncontrollable shudder wracked her body.

"Look at how beautiful she is, Berke." Jack's words were followed by a vibrating growl. "All needy and flushed." He dropped to his knees, bringing his face even with her breasts. He brushed one of her nipples one last time and then captured it with his mouth, sucking it gently. His tongue played over the nub, alternating flicks and gentle licks. "God, you smell so good. Hot and sweet, and that musk is driving me insane."

Berke's talented fingers disappeared, and she whimpered at the loss, her pussy suddenly empty and silently begging to be filled. "Shh…" He moved, hand rising and she turned her head to see him slip his cream-coated fingers into his mouth. "Mmm… I think Jack should get a taste of your sweetness."

A tug on her panties brought her attention back to Jack. He lowered the small bit of black silk and lace to the floor. She lifted her feet so he could toss them aside. Bared to him, to them, she gasped at the flare of animalistic desire in Jack's gaze.

Without hesitation, he lowered his ass to rest on his heels and then brought his face to the juncture of her thighs. He nudged her legs apart and then his mouth was there, tongue delving between her lower lips and tapping her swollen clit.

"Jack!" She leaned forward and gripped his shoulders. The change in position ground her ass against Berke, pressing his cloth-covered hardness into her. "Oh, God."

"Is he talented with that tongue, Gabriella?" Berke murmured, his warm breath bathing her heated skin.

Jack moaned, drawing a groan from her chest, and Berke rocked his cock along the crack of her ass.

"Yes." She panted. "Good." She reached behind her, intent on stroking her mate's hardness, but a hand wrapping around her wrist forestalled her.

"You first, love. Come on Jack's tongue and then we'll take your slick pussy and pretty ass."

A bolt of pleasure zinged along her spine with his wicked words, every syllable adding to her growing desire. Relaxing within his grip, she let her men do as they willed. This one was for her, and she'd be sure to return the favor before the night was through. Later she could suck one into her mouth while the other slid into her from behind. Or lay them side by side while she pleasured one and then the other with her tongue.

Yesss… Those were very good ideas.

Or she could…

Jack sucked on her clit, tugging on the nub, and the action had her body jerking in response, muscles contracting with the ecstasy of his ministrations. He repeated the caress and she responded, twitching once again.

"Shit. There." Jack shoved two fingers into her pussy, and she gasped. "Jack." Only Berke's hold on her hips kept her from falling forward.

Those digits pumped in and out of her sheath, tracing her inner-walls with every thrust and retreat. She rested her back against Berke, leaning into him and trusting him to keep her vertical. With one less worry, she let her gaze center on her kneeling Jack. As he continued his torment, he tilted his head back and raised his gaze. His yellow orbs were focused entirely on her, fierce need written in every line of his features.

Those fingers continued at a maddening pace, matching that of his tongue. The steady rhythm nudged and pushed her toward the edge, shoving her along the path to release with no chance for retreat. She rocked in time with his attentions, shifting and rolling her hips in order to capture any snippet of pleasure she could.

She rode his hand and mouth, gasping and moaning, mumbling and murmuring incoherently. "More. Now. Need. Berke. Jack."

Jack's tempo never stuttered with her movements, his growls the only addition to his attentions. God, those growls…

Her pussy clenched rhythmically around him, milking his fingers, and she let passion overtake her. She was so close... So damned close...

"Come for him, Gabriella. Come and then we'll make you scream." One of Berke's hands abandoned her hip and pinched her nipple, the bolt of pain giving her what she needed to jump over the edge.

With a gasping moan, she came on Jack's tongue. Her pussy clamped down on his invasion, squeezing him tight while pleasure poured through her like lava. Bliss mingled with ecstasy as it roped its way through her limbs. She twitched and jerked, muscles no longer her own, but belonging to the overwhelming joy.

Gabby's release rose and fell with every breath, Jack forcing her pleasure to crest and ebb until she broke down into begging sobs. "Please. Too much."

Berke's attentions immediately eased, his pinches lessening to gentle strokes. Jack's torment lowered as well, his fingers sliding free in slow increments as his tongue gave her tender licks.

Moments passed, and her panting slowed until she could breathe once again. The previously overwhelming ecstasy lessened to a rolling arousal, small tremors attacking her muscles, but at least she could stand on her own once again.

With one last kiss to her mound, Jack rolled to his feet, lips and chin glistening with her juices. "You are delicious, sweet."

Berke gave her a hug, his arms around her waist tightening gently. "Yes, she is." He nuzzled her neck. "Shall we claim you now, love?"

The words were said without an ounce of pressure, but she could hear the suppressed need. Everything in her urged her to say "yes", but kernels of doubt remained. She'd gone through this before. Well, not *this*, but how many men had she been with that told her how much they wanted her and then decided that her curves were too much? Or that she wasn't enough for them? Or that making love to her was like...

Jack's gaze was still intent on her, his eyes searching her face, and he must have seen the indecision in her features. He reached up and twined their fingers together, giving them a gentle squeeze. "You owe us nothing, Gabby. Nothing. But know that whether we mate today or a year from now, we will always want you."

Berke gave her a soft hug to comfort her. "Always. Your Mark told us you were ours, but it's *you* that we want."

Tears stung her eyes as the truth of their words sank into her soul. She had only one answer for them now that some of her fears were laid to rest. There was no telling what the future held for the three of them, but she didn't doubt that they belonged together.

Taking a deep breath, she gave them what lingered in her heart. "Mate with me."

*

Berke took no time in slipping Gabriella's bra from her shoulders, completely stripping her. As she crawled onto the

91

bed, settling in the middle, he and Jack did the same. Once nude, they surrounded her, one on each side of her curvaceous body. Her breasts were lush mounds, her waist slightly dipping and then flaring to her wide hips. Hips that would first cradle them, and then their pups. He couldn't wait to see her swollen with their children, nurturing them within her womb.

He exploited her position, taking his time sliding his palm over her skin, tracing the slight swell of her stomach and kneading her breast. So soft and sweet, a body made to be shared by him and Jack. Their mate. Their soul.

"Are you ready, love?" Berke grazed her shoulder with his lips in a chaste kiss.

"Please?" The scent of Gabriella's arousal hung thick in the air, the musk and honey taunting his wolf.

"On your side, sweet." Jack's voice was wolf-rough, his beast riding the man hard. "Face Berke."

They'd briefly discussed positions, wondering how best to claim their mate. The final bite would require some repositioning, but making love to her would be more intimate with Gabriella on her side while they entered her.

She did as asked, turning toward him, giving a gentle, shy smile as a blush stained her cheeks. She caught her lower lip between her teeth, nibbling the small bit of flesh.

Berke stroked her chin with his thumb and pulled. "No biting. That's our job."

Nerves fled from her gaze, replaced by a wide smile, and she rolled her eyes.

Not willing to allow her nerves to reemerge, he pulled her leg up and over his hip, opening her to both of them. The heat of her core drifted to his cock, and he couldn't imagine how she'd burn him once he slipped inside her sheath.

The pop of a bottle of lubricant alerted Berke to Jack's actions. "Ready, love?"

Gabriella nodded and rocked her hips forward, her spread pussy lips brushing Berke's dick.

Reaching between them, he positioned the head of his cock at her entrance, kissing her sopping hole, but not pushing into her body. "Then take me."

It would always be her choice. Always.

Without hesitation she shifted, and then he was inside her, searing wet heat surrounding him with her rippling velvet walls. He groaned with that first penetration, relishing this initial feel of her around him. Never again would they share this "first."

His entire length disappeared into her pussy, slipping deep until his hips were flush against hers. Only then did he take over, snare control of their movements and give them what they both craved.

Flexing his muscles, he withdrew a handful of inches and then slid in once again, giving her a gentle retreat followed by a slow thrust. With every glide of his cock, her pussy trembled around him, milking him with fluttering contractions. Then a slight increase in pressure, a new tightness, alerted him to Jack's ministrations. With his partner's fingers penetrating her, the feel of her core became snugger than before.

Her chest-deep groan was another clue, the sounds of her low moans increasing to heaving pants. Berke gripped her hip, holding her still as they worked in and out of her body, giving her as much pleasure as they could.

"Does that feel good, love?" Because, God, it felt good to Berke. Better than good. Heaven was not located in the clouds, but within Gabriella.

"Yes..." The word burst from her lips.

More moans joined the wet sounds of his body meeting hers.

Berke's balls were snug against his body, pulsing with the need to fill her with his cum. They'd be tied together in a bond that could never be broken. Her for them, and them for her. His heart skipped a beat at the idea of this one woman for them.

"Berke..." She squirmed. "Jack..." A low moan followed and the increased pressure drifted away.

"I'm going to slip my cock into your ass, sweet." Jack's low murmur joined the moans and groans echoing in the room. "Ready?"

"Please, please, please."

Berke had no doubt that they'd be taking their mate together often in the future.

The pressure and tightness of Gabriella's pussy increased further, the slide of Jack's shaft into her ass stroking him. The squeeze tightened until he thought his cock would be crushed, but in moments they were joined as one, a chain that'd be completed at their mutual culmination.

Ready? Jack's mental voice betrayed him, the stress from the need to move reaching Berke with ease.

Ready. Berke nodded, and then it began.

Gabriella was between them, Berke and Jack holding her still, and he was the first to retreat. He slid out slowly, allowing his tightly leashed need to burst free. He let his body truly enjoy her intimate embrace. Her sheath massaged his cock, stroking and milking him.

He retreated until the tip of his cock was all that remained in her core. His balls protested, throbbing with the need to fill her. As he eased back into her, Jack began his withdrawal, their bodies working as one to pick up an alternating rhythm. There was not a moment that she wasn't penetrated by one of them.

In and out, caressing her with their shafts.

Sweat beaded on his forehead. The fight to withhold his release until she was balancing on the edge with them strained him beyond belief.

Low babbling reached him, Gabriella's words flowing into each other as they escaped her lips. Whimpers of "more", "close", "need", and "gonna."

He released another hint of his control, allowing his body to rush closer to coming, until he hung on by barely a thread. Low moans had turned into echoing groans, his own murmured words mingling with Gabriella's.

Jack?

His Alpha partner grunted. *Fuck yeah.*

Berke sensed Jack's nearness to orgasm and reached between him and Gabriella, intent on nudging her over the edge.

It was time.

*

Thank God, it was time.

Gabby squeezed Jack like a fist, her ass wrapped around his cock feeling like nothing ever before. He'd never had a mate before, either. Never thought he'd ever finish his bond with Berke and tie himself to a Marked female.

His, his, his. The past could never be forgotten, but it could be pushed aside in the light of their ties. Emotions swirled, growing and swelling with every slide of his cock into Gabby. She'd done this: bound them in an unbreakable knot.

More than anything, he craved her love.

He pushed into her once again, moaning at the fierce contraction of her hole. She was close, her sobs and babbling increasing until he barely recognized her words. Berke's hand disappeared between his body and hers, and the reaction was instantaneous.

Yes, she was very, very close.

Their bodies were moist, sweat coating them due to exertion, and the scent of their sex lingered in the air.

Jack's wolf howled at their impending triumph. So close, so near to their lifelong goal. Well, the beast's goal. It hadn't ever given up on Jack. Even when he was at his worst, fighting through grief and resolving to never let anyone close, it had pushed and prodded him.

Now he was thankful for his other half.

When the milking rhythm of Gabby's body continued to increase, flowing from one into the next, Jack knew she rested at the precipice.

Jack's balls were about to burst, his cock stimulated until pleasure was easing to pain, and somehow that simply increased the ecstasy of being inside her. He allowed his fangs to drop and lengthen within his mouth as he prepared to sink them into Gabby's shoulder.

The sound of her moans transformed into screams, and her body trembled.

Now, Berke?

His partner's response was immediate. *Now.*

As one, they rolled, holding Gabby while they moved, repositioning their bodies without breaking their maddening rhythm. Berke was now beneath them, Gabby settled in the middle, while Jack loomed above their supine bodies.

The in and out continued, the see-saw action of their cocks driving all of them mad with need. Berke's emotions raged within his mind, and Jack found that his own mirrored the other wolf's.

Want. Need. Desire. Affection. Lo—

They both backed off at that thought. Too soon. Much too soon.

Gabby let out a high-pitched scream, her hole fisting him in a nearly-painful squeeze, signaling her release... And giving him permission for his own.

Fuck now. He sent the words to Berke, sensing his friend's nearness as well.

It took three thrusts. Three flexes of his hips before his life once again was forever altered. Twice in the same day.

The sixteen-year-old pain he'd been harboring drifted away, destroyed by the day's events. Looking at Berke, he caught the flash of fang, the emergence of the other wolf's canines.

They both craned their necks, teeth resting against Gabby's skin, and then they bit. Sweet blood flowed into his mouth, the coppery tang sliding over his taste buds.

With the taste of the burgundy fluid coating his tongue, his orgasm rushed forward. His wolf howled in triumph at the mating bite and then a blinding rush of sensation overtook him.

His prick throbbed, and the euphoria of release enveloped him. With every pulse of his cock and flex of his hips, tendrils of his new bond with Gabby floated into place.

Snippets of her emotions drifted to him, gentle at first, whisper-like hints of her feelings. They grew in strength and frequency with every spurt of his dick, cum filling her delicious ass as the bliss continued. Her dark channel clenched him, and he imagined her pussy did the same to Berke.

Jack roared against her flesh, his beast wrenching control from him. An echoing sound came from his partner and then Gabby's voice rose above theirs. Suddenly the door between them that had been easing open was ripped from its ethereal hinges. Gabby invaded his mind, her thoughts twirling and dancing with his, her feelings making love with those present within him. She drew them together. Berke's presence also took shape inside him. And then the pain anchored in the past was truly gone. The fear vanished beneath her power, the worry and anxiety pulled from him just as she wove them into one.

One last shudder wracked their connected bodies. Gabby went limp between them, slumping against Berke. Jack still supported his weight on his hands, not wanting to crush his new mate. With care, he slid his teeth free of her shoulder, lapping at the wound as he withdrew. Blood trickled from the injury, and he licked up every drop of the delicious fluid. He normally didn't care for the taste, only suffering through it when his wolf hunted, but he didn't think he'd ever get enough of Gabby. He foresaw biting his lush mate regularly. Already he wanted to mark her again, bathe her in his scent so every other male would know she was taken.

Later. He met Berke's gaze over Gabby's shoulder.

Jack nodded. *Later. And often.*

*

Sweat coated Gabby, the moisture cooling from the chilled air, but she couldn't have cared less. Not when she could sense both Berke and Jack within her mind, their thoughts flowing into her in gentle waves. Pure male satisfaction ruled above them all, but she sensed an underlying caring that seemed to grow with every passing breath. She wasn't delusional enough to think it was love, but the foundation had been built and, brick-by-brick, was growing within their conjoined minds.

As one they shifted, the men withdrawing while Gabby settled more comfortably between their bodies. Berke and Jack's hands didn't leave her as their breathing eased back to normal. Fingers continued to move over her skin, palms sliding along her ribcage to just above her pubis and back again. The touches weren't meant to arouse, but simply to continue their connection.

Jack eased closer, leg sliding over hers as he nuzzled her shoulder. When she focused, she sensed nothing but joy and wonder coming from him, a deep contentment that was echoed by his wolf.

Berke shifted nearer as well, his arm wrapping around her waist while pressing a kiss to her shoulder before moving to share her pillow. His emotions were no less deep. Certain aspects shone brighter than Jack's, yet different. His closeness to love worried her since she wasn't sure of her own feelings.

"Shh…" Berke kissed her again. "We have the rest of our lives." He scraped one of his fangs over her shoulder and then leaned in farther to lap at her new mating mark. "Nothing needs to come today. Or even tomorrow. Having you with us is all we need."

Jack nodded against her, his agreement swift.

"Are you upset about Colson?" Gabby couldn't withhold the question. She recalled Jack's reticence at taking his place, and worried that he'd gone along with things and would come to hate her for forcing the issue.

"Never, love." Jack slid his arm alongside Berke's and gripped her hip. "It took you to make me see the truth, and I would never resent you for today's events." He licked the wound he'd inflicted on her. "We were born to lead. Regardless of my fears. Colson will have the best Alpha Pair leading them, and our Pack will be all the stronger for your presence." He pushed up and braced himself on his elbow. "I'm not my father. I wouldn't harm you or Berke if my life depended on it." Jack sighed. "And I accept that we're a deadly race. Hiding from my true self, punishing you and Berke for my fear, doesn't negate the truth. I am an Alpha, paired with Berke, and mated to you. Nothing more. Nothing less."

Gabby looked to her other mate. "Berke?"

"I don't think we'd have been able to finish our pairing had it not been for you. I don't know that we ever would have." Gabby's gaze remained focused on Berke as he spoke, but she felt Jack nod at the wolf's words. "Now we'll have a home with a Pack desperately in need of good Alphas. Even better, it'll be near Scarlet. And if you'd like, Whitney can come live with us. We know how much your sisters mean to you."

"Really?" She couldn't help the wistful tone.

"Really." Berke brushed a gentle kiss across her lips.

She turned to Jack, anxious for one from him as well. "Really."

Gabby sighed and reveled in their closeness. She could do this. She could continue to heal Jack's heart and grow to love the two wolves in her life. Easy.

She wiggled and snuggled into the bed, enjoying the heat of her mates' bodies as she relaxed. Yeah, it was all good.

Another shift of her body and she wrinkled her nose. "Dude. Scarlet was right. Mating *is* squishy."

EPILOGUE

Gabby dragged her not-so-happy, super-tired ass out to the living area of the suite she now shared with Berke and Jack. She hurt in spots she didn't even know existed, but damn, it'd been worth it. Her mates had taken her places she'd only ever dreamt of and beyond. Just remembering that last orgasm sent a shudder of renewed arousal through her.

Bad vagina. Bad. Any more smexy times and you'll break.

Manly chuckles slipped into her mind, and she gave the men a mental frown.

The soft *thump* of feet approaching drew her attention to the stairs which led to the Ruling Alphas' suite. In moments, a smiling Scarlet and Whitney appeared.

Scarlet threw her hands in the air. "Whee! It's good to be mated to the Ruling Alphas. I get to show up whenever I want, and you can't tell me no!"

Well, at least Gabby was clothed. She looked down at the oversized t-shirt she wore, noting a few holes here and there. Yeah, she'd gotten a little impatient when she'd stripped Jack last night. But her pink bits were hidden, so whatever.

Whitney followed behind Scarlet, a covered tray in her hands, and Gabby perked up. "Breakfast?" Her stomach rumbled. "With lotsa sugar?"

Scarlet gave her a "duh" look. "And coffee is on its way. I stole this stuff from my suite, but carrying burning hot things is beyond me this early. Our new Captain of the Guard is sending one of the 'young pups' along with it. Apparently catering to my every whim is some sort of hazing ritual now."

Yeah, Gabby could see that.

Whitney plopped onto the couch. Gabby soon followed, while Scarlet curled up in a chair opposite them. The Wickham triplets together again. At least Gabby's new home was near Scarlet's. Now they had to figure out Whit's situation.

Snaring a Danish, she bit into it and poked at the big neon yellow elephant in the room. Pink was so passé. "So, I'm mated. And you're mated." She pointed at Scarlet then turned to Whitney. "The question is: what's up with you?"

Whitney's eyes widened and her cheeks flushed. "I don't know what you're talking about." She chomped on her pastry.

"Uh-huh."

Scarlet snorted. "Right. You weren't practically humping the Wardens' legs last night. Sell me a bridge."

Whitney scrunched her nose. "Okay, they're hot, but they're not an Alpha Pair, and I'm not a Marked. No matter what, it'd be sex and nothing else."

Gabby grinned. "Hot sex though." Twin growls filled her mind, overpowering any other thoughts. "Quit it you two!" The sounds quieted.

"Getting snarly, are they?" Scarlet chuckled. "Yeah, we can't talk about guy hotness or sex with anyone but them anymore. Sucks, but true."

"Ugh. Fine. So, Whitney, why were you eye fucking Emmett and Levy? You know, the two non-hot, non-sexy Wardens?" Gabby only got low grumbles from her mates for that one.

Whitney refused to look at her, flicking a crumb off her jeans instead. "I have no idea what you're talking about."

"Liar." Scarlet said the word at the same time as Gabby.

Whit sighed and turned to them. "What did it feel like when you realized that you'd found your mates? I mean, besides the Mark stuff. I'm talking about everything else." So much vulnerability filled Whitney's voice that Gabby just wanted to hug her sister close. "Because… Because maybe…maybe they're mine?"

THE END

If you enjoyed Gabriella, please be totally awesomesauce and leave a review so others may discover it as well. Long review or short, your opinion will help other readers make future purchasing decisions. So, go forth and rate my level-o-awesome!

By the way... you can check at the rest of the Alpha Marked series on Celia's website: http://celiakyle.com/alphamarked

ABOUT CELIA KYLE

Ex-dance teacher, former accountant and erstwhile
collectible doll salesperson, New York Times and USA
Today bestselling author Celia Kyle now writes paranormal
romances for readers who:

1) Like super hunky heroes (they generally get furry)
2) Dig beautiful women (who have a few more curves than
the average lady)
3) Love laughing in (and out of) bed.

It goes without saying that there's always a happily-ever-after
for her characters, even if there are a few road bumps along
the way.

Today she lives in Central Florida and writes full-time with
the support of her loving husband and two finicky cats.

If you'd like to be notified of new releases, special sales, and
get FREE eBooks, subscribe here:
http://celiakyle.com/news

You can find Celia online at:
http://celiakyle.com
http://facebook.com/authorceliakyle
http://twitter.com/celiakyle

COPYRIGHT PAGE